More
Than
Seven
Watchmen

Helen Norris

ZONDERVAN PUBLISHING HOUSE • GRAND RAPIDS, MICHIGAN

Published by Zondervan Publishing House,
1415 Lake Drive, S.E., Grand Rapids, Michigan 49506

Library of Congress Cataloging in Publication Data

Norris, Helen, 1916–
More than seven watchmen.

I. Title.
PS3527.0497M6   1985   813'.52   85-2517
ISBN 0-310-45470-0

Edited and designed by Judith Markham

Printed in the United States of America

85 86 87 88 89 90 / 10 9 8 7 6 5 4 3 2

For my son

"A man's soul is sometimes wont to bring him tidings more than seven watchmen that sit on high on a watch tower."
—*Ecclesiasticus*

"For as long as I am ignorant that the World is mine, the love of God is defective to me.

"Who can love anything that God made too much?"
—*Thomas Traherne*

I t came to pass that on the twenty-second day of December the rector of Saint Stephen's entered the fifty-seventh year of his life. It was accomplished without ceremony. His mother had lived with him for many years, but since her death there was none to arrange these celebrations. The festivals of the Church he served had become the festivals of his life. And this, he felt, was as it should be. The Church year, with its changing colors and memorials, both sad and joyous, had become his year. He had seen it even as a mark of grace that he was born so nearly on the day his Lord was born.

That morning he had risen at seven as he always did, and had gone about his day as if it had been any other. Now, after a modest supper, prepared early by his housekeeper and left to lose its savor in the warmer of the stove, Tom Beckett sat alone in his study in the shadow of the bell tower and wrote his sermon for the service he would hold night after next.

Before him on his desk stood a small-scale model of the church and rectory; the architect had given it to a previous incumbent. Tom sometimes wondered if he should be able to write at all if he did not have before him this slight but sound reminder of his ministry. When his thoughts began to stray, as they did too often now, from the business of the sermon, he found it useful to turn his eyes upon the miniature replica before him, even to reach out and touch the tip of its tower in which the bells could just be seen, or to stroke its tiny roof fashioned cleverly of a substance that was almost slate itself. It was all quite perfect. The walls had the mellowed honey look of age. Even the right transept was traced with fabric ivy. Wonderfully, through the years, the living ivy had patterned the living stone beyond his window in such a way. It was helpful to place his finger at the eastern end on the low-lying portion that served as the rectory, to touch perhaps the spot in the shadow of the tower where this very room would be, where now he would be sitting and writing these words to be spoken on a certain day inside this very church. Then he would put aside the saintly father whose work had set him dreaming and draw toward him the Gospels with their plain and solid words.

Tonight the rectory was full of sighs and stirrings. The roof was settling, the timbers shifting into winter. The crevices around the windows deepened to admit the rawness. The snow had come and with it, cold, and then a chilly dampness. He flexed his aching knee three times, then took his glasses off, and stroked his face. The smell of ink was on his fingers, so strongly that he knew the acid taste of it and drew his hand away.

An unexpected, restless urge possessed him. He walked into the kitchen and drew a glass of water and drank it slowly. When he set the empty glass upon the counter, there ripened all at once a fleeting sense of not being alone. Motionless, he stood and savored it in faint surprise. Then he went into the darkened living room and waited, curious, alert to find the words for it. It was a little as it used to be when he was in his study reading while his mother lay asleep in her room upstairs. There had been her sleeping presence like a hand that never touched him, like a hand withheld, yet just beyond the page he read. In truth, it was a thing that he had never been aware of till her death four years ago withdrew it, and the absence of it sometimes struck him.

He drifted back into his study. He was thinking it was even like the Christmas when his little horse was given. His father with the greatest care had put a blindfold on his eyes and led him out into the cold, crisp air and told him he must guess his gift. And suddenly in the world, without a sound, there was a strange new presence. He could not find a name for it, but to the whole wide dark behind his eyes, it gave a meaning.

He had not thought of that for years. He stood quite still and asked himself if it was what he wanted for a Christmas sermon: In the world a strange new Presence, . . . In the dark a Meaning, . . .

He settled slowly at his desk. When he found his pen, the sense of presence retreated. Again he was alone with words, as he had been for years.

And now he could not quite begin. Once more his hand had sought the church. His fingers, lingering on the roof, just touched the little tower. At once there came the faintest resonance, a deep cave-whisper, a sound as if the wind had stroked the great-C bell in the tower above him.

Startled, he drew his hand back swiftly. Then he smiled,

because he had just read the sound in one of his books. He turned a page. There it was. It was Tauler who said it: "Let the tower with all its bells fall on thee, . . . retreat thee into thy nothingness." And it seemed to him a beautiful thing that in the fifty-seventh year of his life he should read the sound and then hear the echo. Could it be the compensation for growing older, that a kind of completeness at last became possible? One thought of the bell and one heard the sound. . . .

The telephone rang, as if to protest that he could not escape a good round peal. It brought him the voice of Bill Ryder, his curate: deep and pleasant, but hesitant, boyish, a little shy. It was not a voice, Tom felt, for a sermon, though it had its suppressed yet disturbing charm. It began a thing and invited you to finish. And before you knew it you had talked too much. He supposed it was why Bill was good with the young.

"I wanted to pick up the sick list," Bill said.

"Of course. Of course."

"I'll be around in a minute if that's all right."

"Yes, yes. Come by."

He got up from his desk to walk around the room. If he was still for any length of time, his left knee, injured long ago, gave him discomfort. He stood on his right leg and flexed his left knee slowly, holding the stem of the floor lamp for support. Always on Sundays before his morning service he performed this little ritual. Once, lately, Mrs. Travis had burst in with her broom and caught him on one leg like a pensive crane. "Come in, Mrs. Travis," he had called to her calmly as she was slowly backing out of the room. "I'm doing my mission work." And when she had halted, "I have one knee that was never converted. I'm persuading it to kneel at the service this morning."

It was his private paradox that as his heart, with years of

12

turning Godward, fell ever more easily into prayer, it became increasingly more difficult for him to kneel. He must reckon with the sharper pain the years brought to his injured knee. Sometimes he wondered, with a little inward smile, if the painful prospect of arising kept him longer at his prayers. At the end of them, especially when he was not alone, he made a brief, apologetic, silent supplication that he might rise without too great display. Have faith, he told himself. Haven't I always gotten up? And lo, this one more time the Lord assisted him!

But seeing the look in Mrs. Travis's eye—a look of semi-approval, of lending her ample flesh to his gaze and yet of retreating down corridors of time—seeing this look he had encountered before, he stared at the broom, which she held in her hand like the staff the bishop bore in ceremonial procession. He understood her mission. It was, though it was never spoken, to erase from the rug the tracks he made in pacing back and forth before his desk. On Saturday nights he wrote his sermon while he paced. He sometimes wondered if Mrs. Travis believed he executed some wild dance before the Sabbath and that with her broom she covered up a pagan secret of his soul. As he had stood and watched his footsteps disappear beneath her violence, it was somehow to see all traces of himself disappear, . . . the labor of his ministry perfectly erased.

"Mrs. Travis," he had suddenly said, "I have never expected you to sweep on Sundays." Two years ago she had come to him "unsaved," as she had said, and he had swept off her soul a bit and baptized her at her own request between lunch and supper. But some of the mechanics of being a Christian he had failed to impart.

And she had looked at him with her semi-approval. "The dust falls on Sundays the same as always."

He thought of the disarrangement that followed in the

wake of her daily ritual—since her last invasion he had been unable to put his hand on the *City of God*—and the smell of the oil she used on her dust rag, so that even his sermons smelled faintly of oil overlaid with dust. When he opened his notes for the morning sermon, he was sure they could smell it far back in the pews.

"Mrs. Travis," he had sighed, "there is nothing particularly wrong with dust." And when she stared him down, "The Lord, you remember, made Adam of dust. I have always had something like a sacramental view of it."

Now, defiant of making his tracks in the rug, he walked out to unlatch the front door for Bill Ryder. Returning, he seemed to hear again the deep cave-whisper of the great-C bell. He paused behind his desk and waited. Suddenly he switched off the floor lamp beside him and went to the window. He pulled back the drapery and stared through the hickory limbs into the night. For a fugitive moment, high up in the tower he glimpsed a light, so fleeting he could not be sure of its place.

In the dark, he groped for a jacket that hung in the closet and put it on. He went out quietly and stood in the damp, cold air and looked upward. The tower was dark. The moon was behind it, and it seemed to him that what he had seen was a shaft of it piercing the openings in the bell room. But even as he thought to wonder how moonlight struck the bell, the narrow windows of the clock room underneath took on the faintest glow.

So I have a neighbor for the night, he thought with a mixture of charity and amusement. What kind of neighbor would it be? Someone who sought a shelter from the cold . . . or from the law? How did he find the key? he wondered. The key to the tower was kept hanging on a nail behind the door to the basement. He looked across the iron railing and down the moonlit steps until they disappeared in darkness.

His impulse was to descend the steps and determine in the dark if the key were there. But the wind had risen, and in the damp air his knee began to ache, like a faint reminder. Often the very thought of steps was sufficient to bring on the warning pain.

He stood for a moment looking past the tower at the starlit sky, and then down and beyond to the traces of snow gleaming yellow in the light from the porch of the church. Everything had been late this year. The trees turned late. The cold was late. Even the nuts, against natural law, had clung all fall to the hickory tree and now in the rising wind were pelting his roof. For the past two nights they had disturbed his sleep.

He glanced again at the tower and shivered and walked back quickly into the house. When he switched on the lamp in the study again, he could no longer see the faint glow from the clock room.

The presence in the clock room cast a shadow on his mind as he settled in his chair. It surprised him to discover what it was he was thinking: that all the evening long he had somehow felt its shadow.

In the twenty-seven years that he had served this parish, no one, he believed, had spent a night in the tower. He himself had slept closer to its bells than any other. And sometimes when he could not sleep, their weight had been oppressive. "Let the tower with all its bells fall on thee, . . ." Had he just read those words? Or had he always known them?

He shuddered. And it seemed to him the presence in the tower shuddered with him or had shuddered before him. Sitting in the amber circle of the light, he shut it out. And grimly now, with vague unease, he tried to be the bearer of the tidings. . . .

On Christmas Eve he never gave a proper sermon, only

15

what he liked to call A Comment. It had become his custom to begin, "As always on this night," and go on to express his own joy at the joy he saw reflected in their faces. Sometimes he wondered how in fact he should begin were he to look upon them and not see that joy. For all his Christmas words were based upon it. Each year he hung above it a fresh green comment like a wreath.

He stroked the tiny roof for reassurance. Perhaps because it lately seemed—tonight it seemed—that after twice a thousand years the great joy was a pale reflection in the world, only a decent sort of cheer, . . . only a well-trained choir singing carols, . . . only a jolly whiskered figure on the corner ringing bells.

Sometimes now, deep in his heart, he saw himself too clearly. There must be joy. Since Christ had come, there must be joy. With a kind of calculation he placed it in his sermons; he watched them when he spoke the words. If he saw it in their faces, it was given back to him, and at once he could find that joy in his heart. And finding it there, he could give it again. So it was that he had a trick of repeating himself, of throwing out to them a phrase with every art of voice and inflection, of watching it strike and come back to him, of feeling it settle into his heart. And there in his mouth was the phrase again, fuller, deeper, always purer.

In a way, he preached for Tom Beckett alone. The knowledge of it lay in the depths of his mind, beneath all else.

The doorbell startled him, until he remembered. He cracked the window behind him and lowered his head. "Come in, Bill. Come in. The door is open."

In a moment Bill Ryder entered—boyish, tanned, with a head of roughed-up yellow hair, which looked well enough on the playing field across the street but, topping the vestments, was lacking in seriousness; hair that somehow, as

16

Bill bent over the Gospel on a Sunday morning, especially as it usually was in need of trimming, was like a field of oats before the harvest.

"Sit down, Bill. Sit down."

"Well, I'd better not. I left Alice in the car."

"Alice?"

Bill smiled at him and said, "The girl I'm planning to marry, you know."

"Oh, yes. You told me. I see. I see. Well, sit for a minute." When his curate was seated, "Well, Bill," he continued, "what's on your mind?"

Bill looked at him with a small surprise, which was quickly smothered in the gray-blue eyes. His eyes, Tom had observed, were always intensely, annoyingly hopeful, always expecting more than one intended to deliver.

Bill cleared his throat. "You know, . . . the sick list?"

"Yes, . . . yes," Tom said. "I forgot for the moment."

He looked at the young man sitting before him. Always there was a kind of resignation between them, as if they met, but not quite, and accepted the failure. Why there should be the failure, he did not know, since they were one in their desire to know God and to serve man through Him. Perhaps, he thought, it is the cleavage between the generations.

Here was an earnest, personable young man. But if Tom could have put his finger on a flaw, he would have said that his curate was overly ambitious to know God. He wanted to know Him all at once, without the slow seasoning in His friendship. He wanted to serve Him all at once, with some stupendous act of sacrifice or dedication, without the tedious, often painful details of service. "Wait . . . wait," Tom wanted to say to him, "and it will come."

Bill's glance went around the room and halted at the desk. "I'm afraid I interrupted you."

17

"Not at all. Oh, not at all! I was touching up my comment for the midnight service."

"I wanted to get the sick list, that was all."

"Oh, yes, I have it here. . . . Well, it *was* here. Mrs. Travis makes free with my things. Nothing is sacred to Mrs. Travis. Her cleaning hand is indiscriminate. . . . Wait, here it is." He scanned it with his eye. "Why do people insist upon getting sick for Christmas? Afterward, yes. The let-down after all the frenzy. But I should think—" He counted silently. "There are twenty-six."

His voice was not unsympathetic, only a little puzzled. Then he held the paper at a good arm's length and lifted his glasses to see beneath them. "There are several here—I don't believe I recall the names."

He removed his glasses abruptly then, just catching a look in his curate's eye. "But the faces—of course I would know the faces."

He tossed the paper onto the desk. "I suppose," he said, "you know them all."

Bill rose and stepped to the desk and stood looking down at the list of names.

"For example," Tom began as he pointed to the list, "this Mrs. Leverett. And this Ada Leverett. Are they related?"

"They are mother and daughter."

"I don't recall—"

"They don't come to church. They have a . . . something. It's a bone thing. Arthritis, I imagine. Though nobody's sure."

"Both? In one family?"

Bill nodded.

"You call on them, then?"

"Every week, at least."

"Yes, . . . yes," said Tom. "That's very good. That's what we want." And he gave his curate an approving nod. "It's the work of redemption. It must be done." But he said it

18

somehow with an air of abstraction, as if he recalled it from another time. "You're a help to me," he sighed. "You're a very great help. Have I told you that?"

Bill Ryder grinned at him slowly, then sobered. "You said, when I came, you expected me to be."

"I was right about it. When was it you came? Two years ago?"

"Two years and three months and fifteen days."

There was suddenly a brief little silence between them.

"You make it sound so much like a sentence."

"No," said Bill, "I don't mean it like that."

"Bill," said Tom Beckett after a pause, "before I came here I was curate for three years. The calling on the faithful can get a bit dull."

"It's not dull. It's not dull at all. I like it," Bill said. "It's not that at all."

"Well, what is it, then?"

"I like it," he repeated. "It's not anything." His face was flushed underneath the tan, and he swept his hand through the ends of his hair.

Tom sighed. "I want to keep you." His voice was wistful, but tired and even a little impatient. "Why don't you find some nice girl and get married? . . . Well, what is it?" he asked. "What's the matter with that?"

Bill cleared his throat. "You keep forgetting . . . I'm engaged to be married."

"So you are. So you are." And after a pause, "It's the one, I suppose, that you have in the car."

"The very same."

"Yes, . . . yes," said Tom Beckett. "And what was her name?"

"Alice Martin."

"Yes, . . . yes."

Again the silence was falling between them while they

stood together looking down at the list; together but separate, with a space between them that no words could fill.

The knowledge of that space was in Bill's voice. "We're hoping you'll perform the marriage," he said.

"It will be a privilege and a pleasure, I assure you." Tom drew away. His curate always smelled of being freshly shaven. Perhaps the young woman in the car required it.

"We were hoping to see you at the Young People's Christmas. She came along and I put her to work."

"I see. . . . I see. And that was today. There was something, you know, . . . I didn't make it. Did it turn out well?"

"We had quite a time."

"I see. . . . Well, it must be the last of the parties."

"You got some presents. I left them under the tree."

"Did I? Well, it was thoughtful of them." He looked at his curate with a wry little smile. "Fruit cakes," he said, "and handkerchiefs, of course. It frustrates them so when they can't give a tie. But their mothers bake. I sometimes think that my ministry has been to the women who bake. The cake I've consumed in thirty years, . . . the restless nights. However, my digestion is not what it was. It's why I have you . . . to help with the cakes."

Bill Ryder laughed.

"This young woman I hope has a stout digestion."

"She's always hungry."

"I see. That's good. Do I sound ungrateful?"

"Well, really you do."

"I suppose I've reached the age of open ingratitude. There comes a year when you are no longer required to call cake a blessing."

Bill watched him, eyes faintly narrowed, with a trace of a smile.

When Tom was like this—genial, with a glittering edge to

his voice—they were closer; indeed they almost met. And often, deliberately, they both prolonged it. But then it was fragile, insubstantial stuff. Somewhere, far off, something real had sounded, and this was the echo; it could not be held.

Tom suddenly thought of saying aloud that today was his birthday. But after all—"This young woman," he inquired instead, "you have known her for some time?"

Bill glanced at him and then down. "Not long," he said. He paused, shy of saying it. "But it seems . . . I guess it always seems to be so much longer."

Tom looked away. He was conscious that happiness made his curate bold, that Bill trembled even now on the brink of a confidence, that some movement of joy swelled and overflowed. And Tom drew back, as if it were something he could not encounter.

"I suppose so," he said. His voice was strained and a little remote, as if from a distance he watched his retreat and did not approve; as if he regretted it yet was powerless to turn.

In the silence the bell in the tower had whispered, or it seemed to him so: that sighing, whispering, it filled the room. He glanced at Bill to see if perhaps he had heard it too. But the face of the young man betrayed no sign. "Ask not for whom the bell tolls," he thought, "it tolls for thee." He shivered a little and walked to the window and closed it again. The jarring movement he felt in his knee. Turning back, he was older; he turned to the fifty-seventh year of his life.

Bill stood there insistently, eagerly young. Always he seemed to be asking for more. An engaging, a generous, self-effacing boy, yet somehow he required, he expected so much. It was nothing he said, but the rebel or the martyr seemed to stir in his bones. Sometimes when the urgency lay in his eyes, Tom was tempted to say it: "Don't tell me. I'm tired. . . ."

"Bill," he said presently, "about the work. About the work. I like to think that we work together. Well, more than just the ordinary meaning of the phrase. That I do what I can. The parish, of course, is larger than it should be. It's high time we split and formed a mission somewhere. But as it is, as it is, you know, . . . I do what I can and you do what you can. I confess the visiting had become a bit hard before you came. And the work with the young people. I have never, you know, been too good with the children. But it has to be done. It must be done. Not of course that the things I do you couldn't do as well. But there must be, there must be division of labor. And I know I can call on you for a service, for an early Communion," and he tapped his knee, "if this hinge should creak a bit much some morning. So far . . . so far . . ." He lapsed into silence, then gave his curate a sidelong, half smiling glance. "This is my time of the year, you know. I confess I shall miss it when retirement comes. I shall miss most the service on Christmas Eve. The midnight Communion, I shall miss it most."

He was smiling fully at the young man now, inviting him for once to look a little deeper, to share something of himself. All at once he surprised a wistful look, a kind of hunger in Bill Ryder's face. Was it a longing to celebrate that midnight Communion? And yet Tom could not be sure. Perhaps it was only a reflection of his own eagerness. We are inclined, he knew, to find in others our own passions.

Nonetheless, he drew back and took in the situation with a sudden dismay. He knew that more and more he was turning to the service of communion and that he kept the celebration of it largely to himself. It was a thing a layman would have smiled at because he could not understand. The important thing of course was that the service should be done. And none was worthier than another to do it. None indeed was fit to do it. God made him fit.

He thought it was the being made fit, by the grace of God, that both of them were hungry for. We are children all, he was reminded. And this is more than life.

For some, he knew—perhaps for most—it was the Easter service. But for himself it was the midnight Christmas service he built his year upon. It grew in richness all the year. Every weekly celebration of Communion, every special celebration, all of them were joined to make it. And for him the birth of Christ became the opening of the flower, petal after petal—glory after glory—unfolding to reveal the heart so dazzling he could not look upon it. In the service two nights hence he would again unfold the petals, bare the heart, tracing small and close within those walls God's timeless birth. There he would stand as he had stood so many times, given grace to do it. And on that night it seemed to him that he regretted nothing, regretted neither loss of wife nor lack of children. . . . Even his sins seemed of small account in the glow of many candles. Somehow he was less and greater than himself—as the shabby room is humbled yet ennobled by the sunrise—for far off, he caught a glimpse of what it had been promised him by Christ he would become.

In his sermons he must watch for the echo in their faces, but here God entered and lifted it from him. Nothing was forced or indirect. Here it was made between God and himself, between God and the others. God alone wrote the joy in their faces. Tom Beckett need not even look for it there.

Now faintly again he heard the bell in the tower. He glanced up quickly and then away. "Bill," he asked, "do you know if the door to the tower is locked?"

"Of course," Bill said. "But I'll check if you like."

Tom said quickly, "Oh, no, don't bother. I was wondering, you know. Sometimes the visitors go rattling around. We keep a key, don't we, behind the door in the basement? In case the electrician—"

"I'll check, if you like."

"Oh, wait till morning."

The young man smiled at him slowly and shyly, some unreasonable expectation, Tom thought, in his eyes. "You know," he said, "that was the first thing you said to me when I arrived. It was night . . . well, late afternoon. Well, I guess I wanted to get started at once. Too fast, I guess. I was tired of the books, and I wanted to get going." He laughed with the hesitant charm that his senior supposed made his success with the young. "You said, 'Wait till morning.'"

"Really?" asked Tom. "Did I say it then?" Almost, almost they were meeting at last. "What was it, I wonder, you wanted to do?"

Bill Ryder shrugged easily, as if the gesture were pleasure. "I don't know. I've forgotten. I probably wanted to ring the bells in the tower."

A shadow came into Tom Beckett's eyes. He waited, as if listening for an echo from the bell. "I think I may always have held you back a little. If so . . . you must forgive me. For being old."

"No, you haven't done that. You make me think it over, though. Sometimes," he said slowly, "sometimes it seems so good, you know, that you want to do something different. Different. Crazy, you'd maybe call it."

"So good?"

"So good, the whole thing," and he took in the room, the church, the tower, the world with his hand.

Tom nodded. "It's because you are young. I remember how it was. But after a while . . . you begin to see how the old ways are best, and there's no need to hurry, you'll be around for a while. You begin to see it like that."

"Will I?" Bill asked. And he looked at Tom Beckett with a

question in his eyes. Or was it distrust? And after all they had not met.

"Take the services of worship," Tom went on. "Are they different? Should they be? I pray not." He turned to his curate. "Take Holy Communion. . . . Whenever I celebrate Holy Communion . . ." He paused, because again he saw the hunger in the young man's face. He turned to the desk and picked up the sick list, held it without seeing it, and put it down. "Which reminds me," he remarked, "will you take the ten o'clock Communion on St. Stephen's Day?"

Bill did not answer at once. "I'll be glad to," he said at last. In his voice was a fear that he betrayed his eagerness and, underneath, a small resentment at the movement of his gratitude for something that was his, that was intended to be his, and that had been held in keeping for him overlong.

And hearing this, sensing this, Tom felt the hollow at the pit of his stomach. He reminded himself: When the time for it comes, then it comes. I will not ask him to stay. . . . He turned away to the window. I will not ask him to stay. . . . He is waiting to make it three years, the way I made it three. I managed before he came. . . . And suddenly it seemed to him that when the day should come that Bill Ryder would go, there would be no one left.

But God would be left.

He turned again to find his curate standing near the door with the sick list in his hand.

"I'd better go," Bill said. "I've got Alice in the car."

"Yes, . . . yes. It's cold outside. And give her my regards."

He listened to his curate leaving and then somewhere nearby to the closing of a car door. He will be kissing her, he thought in the silence before the sound of the motor. He turned to his desk.

God would be left. The way He was left after Katherine had died.

It was chilly in the room. He began to walk slowly back and forth before his desk, passing each time the miniature model of the church, of the tower and the rectory, of this very room, where now he was pacing back and forth before his desk. It seemed to him suddenly that if he should stop pacing and could look in, for once, through the window of that room, he would find there a tiny figure of himself pacing back and forth before an even tinier church and tower and room; and that in that room another figure would be pacing back and forth. . . . He would see himself as in truth he had become—infinitely shrinking, yet never wholly gone, as if he were another of those words he had spoken that hung almost visibly in the air before the pulpit and refused to disappear.

It was fancy, of course. Yet sometimes when he preached on Sundays—he had begun to notice it the past year, but it could have been there even longer—he felt in some strange way that he was speaking to himself. His parishioners watched him with the usual attentiveness; later, a few of them made reference to his subject or to a portion of his sermon. Yet in the midst of speaking he had seemed to be aware that in that room he was alone. No, it was not quite like that. He was alone, but only in the sense that when he made a point their faces failed to answer him. They left his words unsigned. Sometimes perceptibly he raised his voice, but then he had the feeling that where he stood, apart, a cloud of words surrounded him, hung above him, almost visible, drifted in the air beside him like breath upon a frosty day, and slowly, slowly disappeared. At times he almost lost himself in the midst of speaking, being suddenly conscious that a phrase that he had spoken moments before still hung before him, still was his. And though he might repeat it, it remained with him till of itself it went away.

He began to be weary in the midst of his walking, but he

did not pause. Often at night he would pace his study, hoping to insure his sleeping when he went up to bed.

He looked at the clock and then at his papers spread out upon the desk. He could not bring his spirit to the sermon at this hour. But he paused in his pacing and found on the bookshelf the sermons of John Donne and copied out, for the back of the bulletin—just to give them something to take home with them to read—a portion of a sermon made for another Christmas some three hundred years ago. It had seemed to him a sentiment appropriate to the season, on the mercies of God, and worthy of revival. But as he copied the words, "He can bring thy Summer out of Winter, though thou have no Spring; though in the wayes of fortune, or understanding, or conscience, thou have been benighted till now, wintred and frozen . . . ," he was suddenly very tired, and he put down his pen.

Then it seemed to him for that fraction of a moment that whatever the Church might choose to call the season, for him it was verily the winter of his life, when nothing came forth from him, when nothing was asked for. And he shivered, whether from cold or from age or from no longer knowing if he held the answer. . . .

When the clock in the tower struck ten, Tom locked the front door and climbed the stairs to his room. He did not switch on the light by his bed, but in darkness he walked across the floor to the window and looked out at the tower. High up, between the bell room and the ringing chamber, through the narrow windows of the clock room he saw again the faintest of glows. To a passer-by it might have seemed a reflection of the lamp across the street or of the light that after dark was always burning on the porch of the church. But to Tom it was unmistakable that a stranger passed the night above him in the tower.

He undressed in the darkness and knelt beside his bed. From the floor the tower filled the window, and it seemed to him he knelt before the tower. He shut it away with his hands and prayed to God the things he always prayed at this hour. Then he rose slowly, grasping the bedpost.

He circled the room to take the deadness from his knee. At last he lay in bed beside the window and looked up at the light.

It would have been a simple, perhaps a reasonable, measure to telephone the police that someone trespassed in the tower. But the tower is a portion of the church, he was reminded. If a man should walk into the church at this hour, he would not be called a trespasser. He would be called a sinner, certainly. So are we all. He would have found his proper place.

And thinking it, Tom Beckett closed his eyes and tried to sleep. But he knew he had not said the final thing. There had been nothing in all of this concerning charity or redemption. Perhaps, he thought, while I am sleeping he is going quietly to hell.

After a while, unmoving, he prayed, "God give him grace." Sometimes at night in the depths of his soul he was deathly wearied that he must be held accountable to God for every man that walks the earth. But so it must be, if their paths had crossed. And so it might be, even, if their paths had not crossed. The weight of this oppressed him, like the weight of the bells.

Again he tried to sleep. Deliberately he formed a little sentence he had read long ago, one he sometimes used to find his way into sleep: "God in His infinite mercy has put a night between our days." But twisting and aching in his bones and in his heart, it came to him how John Donne had put it, saying: "Every night's bed is a type of the grave." And when he turned again, it seemed to him he lay beneath the tower and was at its mercy. "Let the tower with all its bells fall on thee." And he knew that if he fell asleep he would dream of it, as long ago, for months, for years he had dreamed . . .

It was after Katherine had died in another place, another city, when he had first accepted the call to this church. He thought he had come through it. He had given her up. And it was as if he had made a covenant with God that he should have his life without her. He would live it out to the end in His service, and God in turn would grant him peace. It had not wholly been accomplished when he came; he had not wholly given her up, and the peace of God was not yet his. But it lay before him.

He had known before they married that with a crippled heart she could die quite soon. Both of them had known it and had not believed. Life was brimming in him, and he could not find a faith in death. God's very life lay in him. He had found his God so young it was like opening his hand and there He was. And it seemed to him that everything he touched with it must live. . . .

For three months she lived. And then it was as if God slowly closed his hand.

There was never any ending. "Will you sit with me," she asked him, "till I go to sleep?" And he had sat with her until she seemed to sleep. He had gone on sitting, waiting, he told himself, for her to wake. But he could feel the life beside him going out. And life itself, the Flame itself, receded, dipped a little down the wick, and had never since flared upward to its old pointed height. The pattern on the carpet dimmed, the furnishings of the room stood out less distinctly. He felt he did not see as sharply as before. And when her mother passed him, weeping, he did not hear her clearly. Her weeping defined nothing. It marked for him no change nor limit. Something had begun to end a while before, and now it

29

was only continuing to end and would go on ending for as long as he should live.

He thought of Katherine now with a slow, deep sigh that came out of his depths. "My dear," he said, "my dear, my dear. . . ." It was not exactly a way of addressing her, nor a way of describing her. Perhaps it was a way of summing it up: the loss of her life . . . and the loss of his.

He liked to think that with each passing year he became a little more what she had wanted him to be. And yet, what was it she had wanted? He liked to think that he remembered all things concerning her, that he held her image sharply in his heart. But in truth, a veil had fallen before that image. He could recall a smile, a word, a gesture . . . little more; and sometimes in the night he grew afraid that imperceptibly she still withdrew, that year by year he lost her more, until at last the day would come when he would search his memory and find no trace except her name. O God, he then was moved to pray, keep me from too much peace. Leave me a little grief. And then at times he wondered if his heart's great pain had fallen down and lodged inside his injured knee—a ludicrous, degraded thing. All things, he thought, are subject to corruption in this life.

After he had been at Saint Stephen's for a month—ninety-seven days he had lived since her death—just before noon he had gone into the tower. The vestments for the choir were kept hanging on the lower floor, which opened from the transept. There had been some trifling thing about them he had wanted to check. And suddenly he was filled with a desire to climb the steps. He had unlocked the inner door, which he had never entered, and had proceeded up the steps into the ringing chamber, where the tautened bell ropes fell down through the ceiling and were neatly looped to hooks against the wall. It was rather like a maypole, he could not help thinking. He was surprised to see the name of every bell on the wall above its rope. He had been told that a parishioner with a passion for the ancient art of change-ringing, as it was done in England, had made a gift of the bells, and though they had long since been immobilized—only their clappers, now electrically controlled, could be moved—the ropes were retained as a tribute to the donor.

Turning on the ladder, he had read the names of the bells: Alfred, Mary, Charles, Edwina, Walter, Anna, Phillip—all names, he had been told, of children in the family of the donor. The ninth bell named William, the smallest of the lot, was never sounded. Cast in England by skillful hands, purchased from an ancient and impoverished church, it had in fact been baptized in the medieval manner and was possessor of a godfather by the name of Henry Rudd. But when, a costly prize, it had been sailed across the water and raised and settled among the other bells, it was found to have what might be called an English voice, high-pitched, of finer timbre than the others. Another bell was cast to take its place in the scale, and little William was suffered to remain thereafter speechless on high.

All this he had been told or had read among the histories of the parish. It had been of little interest at the time. But now in the half light of the tower, with the bells hanging motionless, invisible above him, he seemed to enter into a world of the bells. The thought of their poised weight was oppressive; the smell of hemp was like a presence in the airless room. He climbed slowly toward the ceiling where the ropes converged a little.

Another door was above him, and he passed into the clock room. The wooden steps had ended, and before him was a ladder. The light was coming through the amber panes of the four narrow windows, and the room itself was waiting in a tender, muted radiance—empty, timeless. Only an iron hook high on every wall marked the resting places of the clocks, whose faces, sculptured on the outside walls, would be telling it was noon. This room—the thought occurred to him—was inside of time and therefore, in a strange way, was free of time.

He began to climb the ladder, till he stood suspended with the ropes surrounding him and passing upward straight from floor to ceiling, their beginnings and their endings lost. He waited for a moment—or was it for eternity, since there was no time?—breathing heavily, more than a little dizzy from the climb. Then it seemed that just above him, in a place to which the ropes were journeying, his name was spoken in love. And he was not afraid, because he knew and loved the voice. It was the voice he had lost.

He began to climb again till, reaching a small trap door at the top, he pushed upward and emerged into a world that echoed so within him that he seemed to have known it or have dreamed it all his life.

The clapper of the great-C bell hung directly above him. His two hands could not have covered it. He had been moved to grasp it, to brace himself against the brilliant light and the clamor of the birds, but he did not yield to the impulse. For the things of this place, the bells around him, seemed never to have known a human hand. Climbing yet farther, he stood among them, an intruder. There were nine of them, ranging downward in size from the great-C bell, all frosted with bird lime, to the smallest, the little William, close enough to touch, shrouded heavily in white, like a stillborn child. On every side, the openings of the tower were covered with a screening of wire, which from below had not been visible. Outside, a multitude of birds beat against it in a frenzy of voices and wings, while within, a bird or two who had somehow penetrated the screen circled from one to another of the openings, calling to the others in a passion for freedom. Around them on the floor lay the bodies of those who had never escaped their prison house.

He had stood without moving. The bird voices slowly became one cry, and the cry was his own. Or was it Katherine's? And the beating wings, echoing, reechoing in the mouths of the bells, merged and became the pulse of his blood. She was outside the tower calling to him, and he was enclosed in the prison of this life, this tower, this blood. Only the fragile screen prevented their encounter.

He did not know how long he stood there alone among the bells in an ecstasy of longing to be rid of his flesh, to break through the screen or to find in it the secret opening through which the birds had entered and which they passionately were seeking to discover once again. He placed his hand on the great-C bell to steady himself, and through its shoulder he could touch their clamorous longing in vibration.

And he turned and fled from this longing in himself, knowing, as he did, that God did not permit it, knowing it was God's decision how long he must remain. . . .

He had never known if he fell by accident or if that deep revolt against his life had sent him plunging to the floor below. He lay in pain on the floor of the clock-room, his knee bent under him. He felt no need to move in the sheltered, timeless place, or perhaps he could not. But he could tell that noon had passed away outside the tower.

The amber radiance shifted slowly but perceptibly to the windows on the west. And it seemed to him that some light had shifted within himself, and that when he should rise and go down the stairs, it would be the afternoon of his life.

And so it had been. He was twenty-nine, but the noon of his life had come and gone.

It was not alone the injury to his knee that put the seal of an elderly clumsiness upon his movements. It was not even that he knew at last he would never give her up, that in a

33

sense he pursued her still where she had gone. It was rather that he was weary of this life and perhaps would never wholly belong to it again.

The sharpness of longing had passed, of course, but deep inside him lay that clear rejection, that sense of having once held this life in the palm of his hand and weighed it and found it less than good, found it, in truth, a little counterfeit. For many years now he had lived it out—used it up, was the phrase he made—in a gentle, though sometimes querulous, but detached good humor. He liked to call this the peace of God. But there were times—when he spoke to a young man on the eve of marriage or counseled with a mother on the rearing of her child—that a cold reluctance gripped him and all but paralyzed his tongue; then it seemed that all the labor of his ministry was to further the illusion that life was fair and sweet.

He turned in his bed now, thinking of his name . . . his name, Tom Beckett. . . .

He was still quite little when someone had told him that he bore the name of an English martyr. "But no, I'm named for my Uncle Tom."

"Well, Thomas Beckett was the name of a martyr. You'll see when you grow up and study your history."

"What's a martyr?" he had asked.

"A martyr? It's someone who died for Christ."

For a long time after that he was deeply afraid that he would die like the other Tom Beckett. Later, much later, he came to believe that it was harder to live for Christ. Through the years since his fall, he had sometimes thought—though he tried not to think it—that it was very much as if that other Tom Beckett should have risen from the pavement, after the henchmen of the king had gone, and limped away, unmartyred, unrenowned, to live out his life half in love with

34

death. Oh, the dullness of being athirst for death and being given instead your life to drink. . . .

He turned in bed again, and yet again. The wind rose. And the hickory nuts, which had clung to the trees beyond their season, began to pelt his roof.

A prayer of John Donne drifted into his mind: "Forgive me O Lord, O Lord forgive me my sinnes, the sinnes of my youth, and my present sinnes. . . . Forgive me my crying sinnes, and my whispering sinnes. . . ."

My crying sins, he thought, . . . and my whispering sins. And which are crying? And which are whispering? In the middle of a night past the middle of a life, who can say?

Between a sleeping and a waking, it occurred to him to wonder what a man who proposed to spend a night in secret in the clock room would be doing to the bell to make it whisper . . . and why. It defied all logic. Passing into sleep, he fell again down the tower and lay on the floor in the place of unreason. Forever and forever, the falling into sleep was a falling down the tower. . . .

*H*e awoke to the clamor of the nuts upon the roof. He was lying on his back. The early sun was striking the amber panes in the lancet windows of the clock room, and for a moment it seemed to him the tower was on fire. He had been dreaming, until the dream dissolved at his touch. Or perhaps it had not been a dream. For he had reached a time of life when sleep is full of moving shadows. Whether stirrings of the past or stirrings of things that might have been, they came together in sleep and were blended into one, so that sometimes he awoke with the wondering conviction that he was more than he had been, that he possessed a kind of wholeness, . . . that Katherine had not died.

This morning it was so. He closed his eyes and sought to hold the sleep in his mind. He would not begin to think. He would not begin to live the life he had been given. But the fire of the windows was in his eyes behind the lids. And a hickory nut fell. And he began his day.

As soon as he began it, the stranger in the tower became a part of the day. Dressing and limbering his knee, he told himself: Perhaps he has gone. But he knew it had not happened. He carried the breakfast laid out by Mrs. Travis on a tray to his study to finish up the bulletin while he was eating, and there it was, surrounding him, the presence in the tower. He put down his pen when he had copied John Donne and tried to determine why this presence should disturb him. He found it in a sense even faintly accusing.

He put on a jacket and walked across to the church to leave the bulletin for tomorrow night on Bill Ryder's desk. It was gloomy and cold, an early winter morning with no one about. The basement hallway smelled of cold ashes, and he did not linger. Going back, he looked behind the door for the key to the tower and did not find it. But of course he did not find it. It was a foolish place to keep it. It deserved to be removed.

He went up the basement steps. He stood in the shadow of the tower and looked up at it slowly, and a chill came upon him at the thought that he would climb it. He would climb it, but why? Perhaps it was no more than a nagging unease that so many names on the sick list the night before had been strange to him. If there should be someone up there in need of Christian charity . . . Or perhaps he was in search of something he had left in the tower long ago.

He shook his head against the dizziness that threatened and looked around him at the winter sky, laced with branches bare of leaves and pebbled with clouds. He was thinking, It will murder my leg. And his knee began to ache. I

38

should wait for Bill. But he knew it was not the leg or any pain of the flesh that restrained him now. He knew it was because he had not climbed the tower stairs for twenty-seven years. He knew it was because he feared to find there again the irresistible longing, the sharp rebellion, and the plunge down the steps into this life he bore ... this existence that had the shape and color of a life. Or perhaps it was, in truth, that he feared not to find it, that he feared to find that even the old longing had departed, and that falling again would be the awkwardness of age.

In the open yard the snow had been retreating from the sun, till now it ringed the tower where the shadow crouched upon it and lay within the sheltering arm of the transept. There was no sign of life above him, except the birds crying out against the screen of the bell room.

He said once again: He has gone. And again he disbelieved it. A strange attraction, that was even like repulsion, drew him toward the tower. He began to tremble slightly. From the cold, he told himself. But when he passed the tower door, it was like entering himself. For the fraction of a moment the cry was in his heart: Is it life or death that will be waiting at the top? If it should be death at the hands of someone desperate in the moment of discovery ... So be it, he thought. It surprised him a little to taste the fear of death. He savored it with a fine, impatient scorn of himself. He could smile. But he was suddenly more afraid because there came upon him, as he climbed, a faint echo of the longing to be done with this life.

He tried to pray for God's will, but at once he was a captive to all that lay about him. It was so exactly the way it had been long ago that he could almost believe that no time had elapsed. The plastered walls were festooned with the very same cobwebs. He opened a door and was in the ringing chamber where the bell ropes were drawn and neatly looped to the walls, and above each loop, engraved on brass, the name of the bell.

Out of breath and clinging to the stair rail, he paused to read each name: Alfred, Mary, Charles, Edwina, Walter, Anna, Phillip—he wondered if the children of whom they were the namesakes were living still—and at last that little William, the godchild bell, born long ago in England and living on in exile in a strange land, unrung.

His eyes followed the ropes till they disappeared above him, and he wanted to remain among these children's names, found again after years. He read them once more, his spirit reaching out with a kind of desperation he could not explain. Suddenly they seemed to him the only names that belonged to him now. He wanted to believe in them, and believe in the children to whom they had belonged.

And all he could believe in was his own strange folly . . . and his own intense reluctance to climb into the clock room.

It no longer seemed important that a stranger was awaiting him. A fragment of a psalm that had come into his mind after Katherine's death was present with him now: "In God have I put my trust, I will not be afraid: what can flesh do to me?" Then it had meant to him his own weak flesh that could sicken with the pain and fall out of faith. Now it meant an unknown treason in his blood. . . .

He climbed up slowly and opened the door into the room above.

In the amber radiance he saw at once that there was no one. His heart was pounding in his head, and he closed his eyes. When he opened them, he saw on the floor in the corner what appeared to be a heap of hangings from the altar—red and green and white. He put his hand upon the ladder to steady himself. Then he walked slowly forward to find a bed made of altar linens, blanketed with the hangings and pillowed with a cushion of red velvet from the pews. Beside it on the floor were seven altar candles.

"O God!" he said beneath his breath. And even as he said it, he gave himself assurance that he took the Name not in vain, but rather called Him to witness the desecration before them.

Not far away were paper cups, a package of powdered milk and one of sugar, and a china saucer. It seemed to him they might have come from the kitchen in the basement of the church. His eyes returned to the bed with a kind of fascination. His mind took note of the fact that it lacked the purple color of the Advent season. At least, he thought, the altar has not been stripped of its hangings. The invasion, it would seem, had been confined to the sacristy, where the linens and the out-of-season hangings were kept . . . and the nave and the kitchen.

As he was deciding this, he felt a touch upon his leg. He leaped backward, banging his shoulder on the ladder. Looking down, he saw a gray striped cat, who was looking up at him with green slanted eyes. She closed them while she stretched her forelegs delicately and thoroughly. She appeared to be expectant, far advanced in the state. She moved from him to wind herself about a bell rope, then slowly unwound and wandered off aloofly to sniff an empty saucer. With an infinite deliberation she turned and walked away to curl herself among the hangings.

Tom closed his eyes. When he opened them again, he saw a heap of feathers on the floor at his feet. And with a further sense of shock he was aware that the cat had gorged herself upon the birds that were trapped in the bell room.

For the first time then he heard the clamor of the birds. He glanced up, and at the summit of the ladder the trap door was open. He was staring into the mouth and clapper of the great-C bell.

41

He grasped the sides of the ladder and began unsteadily to climb. He dared not look down, for fear of being dizzy, and he dared not look up, for fear of seeing more than he could bear at the moment. He kept his eyes on each succeeding rung till he emerged into the light. Then he clasped the ladder firmly and threw back his head.

There above him, astride the great-C bell as if it were some monstrous bird, awaited him, improbably, impossibly, a child—a boy, who looked to be some seven or eight. Tom all but lost his balance on the steps. When he recovered sufficiently to be aware of what he did, he found that he was staring at the small, jean-covered knees clenched against the iron bell sides, at the grimy hands, and at the great brown eyes that took him in, acknowledged him, seemed even, in a sense, to know him.

Unsteadily, his bad leg trembling, Tom retreated to the clock-room floor, as though the child were a fact he could encounter, might even overcome, but on a firmer ground. The cat, brushing suddenly against him, sent a shock through his body, and he glanced down quickly. Then he raised his eyes and cleared his throat.

"Come down," he said.

He sounded more peremptory than he intended. His tone reminded him of the time he had discovered the exterminator sipping Communion wine in the sacristy: "What do you think you are doing, sir?" "Availin' myself of the hospitality of the house." "You're availing yourself of what was intended to become God's hospitality to many more than yourself." And the man had lowered the bottle and stared, not so much at the words as at the voice that shaped them.

For a moment he thought the boy was not going to obey. Then a leg slid over the great bell's shoulder, struggled for a footing on the rim of the sound bow, slipped but somehow retrieved itself while the bell sighed and whispered. The slight figure was descending the rungs of the ladder, the seat of his blue jeans white with bird lime. And now Tom confronted the broad, horizontal stripes of a T-shirt, the navy sweater too short in the arms, the pale hair even more untidy than Bill's and streaked with the fluff from a few gray feathers, the neck that was longer, more slender than most, the small thin face, great eyes, full lips, soft, retreating chin—in short, the disturbing, formed and yet unformed, knowing yet wondering face of a boy. He could hardly say that the child looked afraid; but hungry, yes.

The cat made a loving dive at Tom's injured knee, and he winced. He said in a clear voice that strove to be kind: "What are you doing here?"

The question was a large one for the narrow room; it seemed to rise into the mouth of the bell and echo with another: What am I doing here? And at once he was aware that he should have asked, "Who are you?" Its answer included everything, included even, in the echo, "Who am I?" And after a moment he asked it. "Who are you?"

The brown eyes shifted. The boy bent over the cat and swept his hand along the sleek, arched back and rose with her head tucked under his chin. He looked at the middle button of Tom Beckett's jacket.

"Are you going to answer me?" Tom said at last.

Slowly the eyes traveled up to Tom's own, then turned to stare at the narrow window, catching and holding its amber light and not letting it go.

"Well now, . . . well now." Tom was quite at a loss. And now he was beginning to react from the tension and the climb. His knee was trembling badly, and he felt unstrung, as if the tautened ropes that stretched around him in the clock room had suddenly gone slack inside his chest.

"I think," he said firmly, "you'd better come with me."

The boy made no move, but the cat suddenly leaped from

his arms and went dashing up the ladder—with alarming rapidity, Tom thought, in light of her condition. A small bird was poised upon the sound bow of the bell.

Tom held out his hand. "I want the key," he demanded in his congregation voice—his Resurrection voice, someone had named it. "I want the key to this tower." He might have been calling for the Keys of the Kingdom.

The boy looked frightened, but he did not stir. Above them, the birds were crying frantically.

Tom turned without a word and went down the stairs. When he reached the lower floor, he found a chair that held the music for the choir. He closed the door to the stairway and wedged the chair beneath the latch.

As he went in search of Bill Ryder, it occurred to him that he was trapping another bird in the tower.

In the basement of the church the day had begun. On Wednesdays, till two o'clock, Mrs. Finley kept a nursery school for preschool children, to enable mothers to do whatever mothers wished to do unhampered by their young. It was sponsored by a guild, and Tom had approved it, though he had not really seen the crying need. Sometimes the children managed to elude their keeper, and once he had found a small girl in the rectory bathroom. Her intention was to take a bath, it seemed.

When he entered the nursery now, two small creatures of indeterminate sex and age were coloring pictures on the floor—unwatched by Mrs. Finley, he observed distractedly. She did not seem to be around.

He asked, "Is Mr. Ryder anywhere about?"

The children stopped and looked at him with wide, suspicious eyes. They were hiccoughing not quite in unison, and this unnerved him further. He was not sure they were old enough to talk.

44

He went into the hall and called in sudden desperation, "Bill! Where are you?"

And when the curate came miraculously from nowhere, "Bill," he half complained, "why is it I can never find you? Come in here," he said, "and close the door." When they were closeted in the Junior's classroom, he began, "Something has come up." He could not for the moment find another way to state it. Dimly in his mind was a line from Lewis Carroll, or someone else, which said that what goes up must come down. And suddenly he could not keep from laughing at the sheer stupidity of all this running up the tower and down the basement. Then, seeing the deep concern upon Bill Ryder's face, which must somehow reflect his own, he said quite simply, "There's a boy up in the tower."

"A boy? Well, I'll go up and get him down."

"He's living there, it seems." Tom sat abruptly on a table, on a paper model of the temple at Jerusalem.

"You mean—"

"I mean he's keeping house." Tom paused. "He's fixed it rather nice. You'll see, you'll see." A small hysteria trembled in his throat.

"Well, who is he?"

"He declines to give his name. Or to say a word. Or to come down. He's in the clock room now. Or was."

Bill looked at him in some surprise. "You mean you climbed—"

"Yes, yes, I climbed," Tom said impatiently. "But I have no urge to climb again." He sighed and rubbed his knee with his hand and found that both were trembling. "It sapped my vitals," he said. "You climb."

"I'll get him down." Bill opened the door.

"Bring the cat with you too. He's got a cat. And Bill," he

45

called out. "Wait, Bill. Get the key. . . . He's got the key to the tower."

When his curate had gone, Tom blew out his breath in a weariness of flesh and of spirit. He thought it would be good to go into the church and remain for a while, but such retreats never seemed to be in order when he needed them most. He told himself that once the child was brought to earth, he was in Bill's province. He had a vision of small boys playing tackle in the afternoon across the street. He passed his hand across his face and wished he had a drink of water. But the way to the kitchen was through the nursery, and he did not feel equal to the nursery. Groaning, he got to his feet and kicked his knee and walked up the basement steps.

The sun was warm and white on the gravel walkways. The tower stood in planes of light and shadow. The squirrels were sporting in the branches of the hickory. He drew in his breath. There was a bitter-sweetness in the air that belonged to early winter, as of something promised and not given, or of something given and not taken. And it was in his throat, the bitter-sweetness. It was the light and shadow on the tower . . . and on his heart.

The sun rose, the day advanced, and Tom waited. . . .

He waited, pacing the brown grass before the tower in a kind of shame that he had been so harsh to the child. It was not that he had never wanted one himself. On the contrary, it had once been so sharp a longing that he had not understood it in himself, a man. This longing for a child was said to be a woman's part. But after Katherine died and he knew at last for certain that he would never marry, it came upon him slowly, like a wave from somewhere in his depths, that he would never have a child. And with a deep, disturbed, and secret pleasure he took to watching children playing together. But when he saw a solitary child, he heard a little whisper of reminder, "That is not your child."

46

He still remembered how a woman in his church had sat in his study and wept because she had been told she must be childless. He had no word to say to her; he only turned his head. Not because he failed to understand, as she must have thought, but because the child that he himself would never have had risen between them so full of life and sweetness, so all but alive, that he could not speak. So he sat before the woman, locked with her in mourning for this child, and there seemed to him no words for her or for himself.

But now all that had passed away, like the late snow that had melted, with only a trace left here and there behind the hedges and in the corners that never felt the sun.

Still he paced before the tower, dreading the descent; dreading, for some reason, to confront the child again; hoping, for once, to hear the urgent ringing of the rectory telephone. It seemed to him that with the years his telephone called out with more insistence, and that the voice it brought to him required more, pled for more—more understanding, guidance, peace of mind, involvement. It seemed to him it talked a little longer than it used to talk. It seemed to him it wanted words, not sacraments; it wanted counselings and meetings in his study, in preference to his presence at the altar. It is possible that I imagine this change, he thought, still pacing. As if to underline that possibility, the telephone kept silence.

Into his state of mind the cat descended, stepping from the tower steps with mystery and grace, arching her gray back in the warmth, closing her eyes in pleasure at the sunlight, moving forward, pausing to lift a foot and plant it firmly in the brown grass. Then stretching backward from her front paws, she arched her back the other way till it must break for pleasure in the gesture, and thus she lay upon the grass and waved her tail and drew it comfortably beside her and looked at him with half-closed eyes. He felt that he was

47

dispossessed. He felt that she had seen him through the window of that tiny rectory in his study, ever shrinking, pacing back and forth.

And then the others were upon him. The boy, head bowed, was looking at the cat.

"Yes, . . . yes," Tom said, and he searched his curate's face. "Have you discovered . . . anything?"

"Not yet," Bill said and smiled, but briefly. "It's going to take a little time." And after a moment he asked, "What do we do with him?"

Tom looked at his curate with an uneasy question and a quiver of alarm in the corner of his mouth. "Do with him?"

"I have one room," observed the younger man. He said it with apology, but he said it.

"Yes, . . . yes," said Tom. He looked at the child's head and cleared his throat. "Well, Mrs. Travis will fix him up at the rectory till we can find where he belongs."

"Well, then, I'd better get back to Mrs. Gates. I left her sitting in the office by herself.'".

"Mrs. Gates?"

"She has a problem with the Red Cross."

"I see. . . . I see. Well, of course you must return to her."

He watched his curate take the basement steps. "Bill," he called, "if you would check with me again before you leave. I mean . . . before you go somewhere, if you would check with me—"

Bill nodded. He seemed annoyed or amused. Or was it both? "I'll drop by." He disappeared.

Tom Beckett stood a little distance from the boy. A tiny panic threatened him. His knee gave forth a warning twinge that he was near the edge of something. The boy bent suddenly and picked up the cat, and the two were leagued and proof against him.

"Well, now," Tom said, "where were we?"—as if a

48

conversation had been briefly interrupted. It was a phrase he often used in counseling to make a place for him to stand when he was losing ground.

The boy looked up at him, then ducked his head.

"Perhaps I should tell you that I am a minister, and this is my church. And over there is where I live. But of course you are old enough to put things together. . . . Do you ever go to Sunday School?" He was matter-of-fact.

The boy nodded slightly.

"I am very glad to hear it. But of course I won't ask you where it is you go." And he smiled. Or he began to smile. But he found that he was looking straight into the eyes of the child, and it seemed to him there was a way of looking at one another that was neither smile nor lack of smile, but something suspended, as it were, between the two. It was a waiting to smile. There is no hurry, it said.

"Well, now," he said, "shall we be friends?" Still he looked at the child. And suddenly it was the most hollow phrase he had made. It was the phrase from the pulpit that hung in the air and would not disappear. It was the Comment on Christmas Eve, the way it could become. Perhaps this Christmas Eve, if the answering joy should fail him.

It was hot, and he looked up and saw that the sun was nearly overhead, that it was almost noon.

"Well," he said, "we shall just go and tell Mrs. Travis to put another plate on the table." He began to walk ahead. For a moment he could not be sure the child was following. Then he heard the footsteps on the gravel behind him.

When he opened the door, he remembered that after breakfast he had promised Mrs. Travis the day off to go Christmas shopping and that he had a luncheon engagement with his senior warden.

While the boy sat and held the cat in the living room, he

went into his study and gave the man a ring. "My apologies. I can't make it. Something has come up."

"Something has come down," would have been more exact, but that would call forth questions. It was engaging how a tiny word could settle things. If he said "up," that ended the matter. But if he said "down," the fat was in the fire.

He hung up and dialed his curate's office. The woman with the Red Cross grievance went on talking after Bill had answered. "Bill," he said in lowered tones, "you'd better call the police and just fill them in. I'd do it, but I'd better not alarm a certain party." He felt distinctly foolish, and he could sense that Bill was grinning at the phone. He hung up abruptly when he thought he heard the sound of a door, then discovered it was only that the cat had knocked an ashtray from the table.

In the living room the child was looking at the floor. With a kind of hesitance Tom tried to read the narrow face. Everything was locked away but hunger.

"Are you hungry?" he asked. The small head was shaken in denial. "Come now," he said. "Come now. We'll find something in the kitchen." His heart sank all at once at the thought that the child had spent the cold night in the tower in his light apparel. But then the altar hangings—the red ones and the green ones were of wool. He winced a little at the thought of them. They must be gotten down, he thought. I must speak to Bill. . . .

While he led the way to the kitchen, he felt a tremor in his knee as of foreboding. He opened the door of Mrs. Travis's refrigerator—he always thought of everything in the kitchen as belonging to Mrs. Travis—and left it open while he brooded into it. Then he took out everything that it contained, except the vegetables and the cartons of raw meat, and placed the items on the kitchen table.

50

"Sit down," he said to the boy. "Oh, you'll need a plate." He found a plate and a fork and knife and a glass for milk. He studied some saucers of leftovers briefly. "We could heat these," he said, "but I doubt if it would help them." He sniffed at one of them, reflecting on the nature of leftovers, and then on the twelve baskets remaining from the feeding of the multitude, wondering if they had been found superior to other leftovers. But a miracle is a miracle, and doubtless that had been a part of it.

The cat came from under the table and slid against his leg, and then against his other leg, circling him in a slow, deliberate ritual. He drew the saucer of uncertain contents from under his nose and filled it with milk and placed in on the floor.

"I'll eat a bit later," he explained when he had straightened. In truth, he discovered that the climb in the tower or the presence of the child had quite taken his appetite. He could not recall having eaten alone with a child in his life. Groups of them, of course. Church School picnics. But not a solitary child.

He left the boy to eat and went to his study. There he paced about, pausing now and then to kick the ache from his knee, which the climb in the tower that morning had brought on. Yet he was aware that it was not the climb alone, but that his knee had absorbed what had been waiting at the top, and even foretold what awaited him below, foretold that when he went into the kitchen in several moments' time, it would not be easy.

Sometimes it seemed that his injured knee was quite the most sensitive and sensible part of him. It appeared to know things first, before he knew them in his mind, and not alone the changes in the weather, the way his knee saw through the smiling mask of spring to the lurking chill of March, or was aware, before the windy day itself, that it would lie down quietly by afternoon. There were things of deeper import. It heralded a bout with influenza, or small depressions, or a slight misunderstanding with his curate, or a poor attendance at a Sunday service. Indeed he had grown to rely upon his knee and sometimes felt he would not have it whole again at any price. Forewarned is forearmed, he told himself, as he flexed and unflexed the knee joint suddenly, taking the sleeping crick by surprise, as if he would kick it across the room.

When he returned at last to the kitchen, he found that he had left the door to the refrigerator hanging open, and that the boy had not eaten any of the food, but sat before it with his eyes cast down to the cat upon his lap.

"Well, now, . . . well, now," said Tom Beckett, and he slammed the refrigerator door and stood looking at the boy. Then he walked to the table and poured a glass of the milk and passed it back and forth beneath his nose, as if judging its freshness. He put it down firmly on the table. "Drink it," he said.

Slowly the boy looked up at him, and his eyes were filled with tears.

"Now, what is it?" Tom asked, and a small impatience stirred in him that was very like despair.

"All right," he said at last, "you don't have to tell me your name. Not now, at least." He took a turn around the kitchen, and the cat jumped down to follow him. He was afraid he would step on her. He said, with a note of pleading in his voice, "If you don't eat something I shall be most uncomfortable. I'm not accustomed to children," he added, "and there is probably something I have handled badly in connection with your situation. But if you will drink the milk I poured and maybe eat a little cheese, I shall be much more at ease with you . . . and possibly more helpful."

He turned away then and stood in front of the window,

peering past the cottage curtains into the ivy on the wall of the church. When he turned back, the boy had the milk in his hand and was munching something else. The cat was on the table, but he did not protest.

He escaped by the back door to find his curate. Bill was in his basement office, but the woman who had come about the Red Cross was lingering. Tom paced up and down in the hallway and paused at intervals before the door, clearing his throat with a sound of crisis. He could tell she was a woman who required firmness, a suggestible creature with a nonexistent problem who could be led to stay or leave according to the tone one used. His curate showed no understanding of the type. One gently interrupted them, one asked if one might have a prayer, . . . one pressed their hand and showed them out. All in the name of Christ, one made a temporary end of it; they would return. God bless them, they would come again tomorrow. He stood in the hall outside the door and mentally supported her departure. In a moment, so assisted, she could say good-by. He told himself, in making her a bow, that it was what she wanted.

When she had passed, he strode into the room. "Did you get in touch with the police?"

"No. No, I didn't."

"Well, why didn't you? Why didn't you? It shouldn't be delayed, you know. I'll do it myself!"

"Well, all the time I was talking to this Mrs. Gates, I kept thinking. And once I excused myself—I want to show you something in the room across the hall."

Bill turned and walked from the room. Tom followed with impatience. In the classroom they entered Bill led him to a photograph thumb-tacked against the wall and pointed to a small face in a double line of faces.

Tom stared. "You mean he's one of ours?"

"Well, isn't that the kid?"

"You mean—?"

"I mean he's in Miss Honicutt's class."

"But then you can find out—"

"I have found out. His name and where he lives. We have him in our files. I described him to Miss Honicutt over the extension in the nursery, and she thought of his name. She doesn't know much about him, except she thinks his father left some years ago. And not long ago—within the year, she thinks—his mother died. And now he lives with an aunt. He's been coming off and on to Church School with the children of this aunt."

"I see, . . . I see," Tom said slowly. "But what I don't see is what he was doing in our tower."

"Well, I guess he ran away. Isn't that what you would guess?"

"Ran away? Ran away? Why would he do that?"

Bill smiled and shrugged. "Why not ask him?"

"Do you suppose he was mistreated?"

"I doubt it." He gazed at Tom with a glimmer in his eyes. "Didn't you ever want to run away?"

Tom suddenly looked down, and after a moment he said, "I believe I was older. Much older, you know." And then he did not quite know why he had said it.

Bill was watching him with interest. "Did you do it?"

"No, . . . no, I didn't. But it wasn't the same thing." And suddenly his knee began to nag at his heart. And a kind of holy fear was in him because it was not the same and yet the tower was the same. Or was it? Were all escapes the same?

He waved his hand and drew himself into his customary testiness, impatience. "Where was he running to? Was this tower the end? In my day, they were joining circuses or hiding out in caves. And before that, they dreamed of stowing away on a ship. But today . . . where is there to go today! Where would you go?" He sounded indignant. "The circus is

54

done for. The caves are now museums." He subsided. "It seems they run up instead of away," and he glanced toward the tower. "I suppose, if I tried, I could find a nice symbolism there. Something for a sermon." He looked at his curate in dejection and sighed. "That's the trouble with our calling. You see everything in life in terms of next Sunday's sermon or the sermon after that. . . . You must resist it, my boy. It is our great temptation."

"I'll resist it," Bill said.

"In the meantime, Bill, you must call this little woman—"

"I have called her."

"Had she missed him?"

"Yes, but she had an idea he was somewhere else. He must have done this before. She sounded pretty tired."

"Not worried, eh?"

"Well, just pretty tired. I told her I'd be around with him shortly."

"Yes, of course. Yes, . . . yes. Well," he said, "I'll just go back and see what he's about. I have a feeling he might take off, now he's had his lunch."

"Why?" asked Bill.

"Why not?" There was something in the way Bill turned his head that rasped Tom's nerves. "Nothing in his manner has suggested repentance. . . . Are there special inducements I could offer? Gold stars for every day he sticks it out at home?" Gloomily he gazed the length of the room and through the window panes that so badly needed cleaning they diffused the sunlight, like the stained glass overhead. "I might wish there were a service in the Prayer Book for fugitives from parental justice, but I find none."

"Except he has no parents."

"Well, now you're quibbling."

Bill shook his head. "No, I'm not. The way I see it . . . that's the point." He swept his fingers through his hair. "I had none either." He glanced at Tom and then away. "Well, in the beginning I mustered a couple. They got away somehow." He was smiling faintly. "It makes a difference."

Tom looked at him with some embarrassment. "Well, now," he said, "you never told me this."

"You never asked."

"Do I need to ask?"

Bill turned away. Presently he said, his voice constrained, "Do you want me to take this kid off your hands?"

The room was still. Down the hall, the children in the nursery began to chant a song.

"You think you could handle it better, perhaps." It was stated, not asked.

There was another silence. "I might get him to talk."

Tom almost said it: Take him, take him. . . . But he drew back slowly. He could smell the bitter-sweetness in the winter air above the basement—the scent of something promised and not given or of something given and not taken. He stood in a deep uneasiness of spirit, as if somewhere there sounded a final warning. . . .

He turned to the door and said it lightly, "I'll give it a try." But he turned back slowly. "I'll need to know his name."

"Timothy Braden. His aunt is a Mrs. Davis on Maple."

Tom said, still lightly, "I see you have committed it to memory."

"I do this for a living," Bill Ryder said.

And they stood there facing one another; smiling, yet in a kind of struggle, Tom thought with a sense of shock . . . as if they would never meet, except in combat. But this is all wrong. . . . This is not what is intended. We are both going the same way, loving the same things. . . . And for a moment Tom Beckett was unsure where he was going and what things he loved. In his confusion, he could almost speak the

56

words: So I have fallen short. I grant you all my failings. But what particular failing is enough to keep us strangers?

He turned abruptly and went down the hall and up the basement steps.

When he walked into the house, he had a sudden fear that it was empty. He stood in the living room and could hear no sound except the ticking of the clock on the wall of his study. He's gone. . . . It is over, he thought. So be it. So be it. And then he could not tell if he was glad or afraid, except that suddenly he had an impulse to go into his study and explain it all to God, . . . explain that he had done the things he knew . . . this day in the fifty-seventh year of his life, when the course was not as clear as it used to be. It was strange, but in his mind the matter lay between Bill Ryder and himself and somehow not between himself and the child. It was easier to explain a thing to God than to Bill. God had listened for years. He could be humble with God . . . but not with Bill.

And then he saw the child standing motionless before the window in the dining room, the cat in his arms. The blinds were drawn, but he held the slats apart with his fingers. The two of them were peering through the opening at something. Tom could tell by the brisk and wicked motion of the feline tail that it would be birds or squirrels.

"Timothy," he said. The boy turned abruptly, and the cat leaped away. Tom had torn apart a world with the name.

"Timothy," he repeated. "You see, I know your name." He walked to the archway of the dining room and stopped. "I'm almost sorry to know it, if it's what you don't want." Then looking at the face, he realized with surprise that the child had known his, Tom's name, all along. And he said, "You knew my name all along, but I didn't know yours till just a minute ago. I will never forget it," he finished simply. It surprised him to have said it. And suddenly it lay no longer between Bill Ryder and himself; it lay, he knew at last, between himself and this child.

"I would like to have you come with me," he said. "Just to the other room." He turned and led the way to his study. And when the child and his companion were inside, "Sit down," he said and pointed to the chair beside his desk. Timothy picked up the cat and sat down.

Tom sat behind the desk and studied the phone book for several moments. Then he dialed. "Mrs. Davis," he began, and he did not look at Timothy, "I am Thomas Beckett of Saint Stephen's Church. . . . I have the boy at my house. If it would be all right with you, I'd like to keep him till tomorrow. Then of course I'll take him home. . . . Thank you, Mrs. Davis. Thank you very much."

When he put down the phone, before he turned and saw it, he knew the look of betrayal on the face before him.

"Timothy." He said it humbly, for he was looking at the face. After a while he ventured, "I didn't ask you first if you wanted to stay with me tonight. It wasn't because I didn't want to ask you or because I didn't think I needed to know what you would like. It was because I was afraid you'd say you didn't want to stay."

The boy dropped his eyes to the cat in his lap.

"I see I was right. But I wanted you to stay. And now you must forgive me for arranging it for you." He found to his surprise and discomfort that his voice was trembling. Again, as in the tower a little while before, the question occurred to him: What am I doing here? To give himself a feeling of belonging in this room, in this place at this time, he reached out and touched the tiny transept of the church on his desk and discovered all at once that his hand was trembling too.

The cat was purring faintly. The boy stroked the fur all the wrong way, then the right way. Tom Beckett looked aside while he tried to recall if he had ever counseled with a child in this room. Or with a child at all. Certainly, but certainly, they had their problems too. But when he stopped them in the churchyard or in the basement hall and asked them how they were, they always told him they were fine. It was an answer he had never grown accustomed to; it seemed somehow evasive. Perhaps because a different phrase had been required in his childhood. There was, of course, the little boy a week ago who had looked up from beneath a ragged head of hair and replied, "My belly hurts." Tom had paused, almost startled, and then had said gravely, "We'll do something about it." He had glanced in both directions down the basement hall, as if for reenforcements, and when he turned back the child had disappeared, leaving Tom with a thrust of the pain so peculiarly his own. Now he flexed his knee, till the whisper of that pain echoed up and down his leg.

He turned back again: this child had not disappeared. With his eyes on the miniature tower, Tom measured the distance between them. Half a century. The thought of it halted him, yet moved him strangely.

"Timothy," he said, "I have a feeling you won't tell me of your trouble because I am older, and you think it won't seem important to me . . . as it does to you."

He hung there, waiting. "You could be very right. Because the things . . . the things you want so much or fear so much will change as you grow older. They will change a great deal—"

He was silent for a while, his eyes on the boy's hand ruffling and smoothing the fur of the cat.

"Do you know," he said, "that yesterday was my birthday? I hardly gave it a thought. But I can remember how it was with me when I was just a little younger than you. I remember there was one year . . . one year I was so full of my birthday I couldn't see the world for seeing myself."

59

The boy's hand rested on the cat's white throat. Noting how it did, Tom came to rest in the past for a moment. And dwelling there, he seemed to touch the troubled mind of this child. He went on gravely—and simply, he believed—but allowing to his voice a little of the eloquence that was almost now a habit when he spoke of the past, any past, of the things that time had drained the heart from, to which a tone, an inflection could restore a kind of life.

"My father told me in the early morning, 'Today you can have anything at all you like.' When I heard that, I wandered over all the house and yard, thinking of the cake and candles first, and then thinking past them to what out of all the world I wanted most to have. And nothing I could think of was splendid enough for the prince of the universe I became for the day. I looked at the tops of the hills and the clouds, and they were made for my pleasure. I looked at my parents and my dog, and they had been created to do my bidding. 'Lie down,' I said to Pal, and he lay down as if he understood what I was.

"And all the time I asked myself, What do I want most? By noon the question was a fire in my breast. 'How much longer do I have?' I said to my father. 'Well, you have the rest of the day, of course.' And my mother said to him, 'You're cruel,' and she smiled at me. 'You'll ruin his birthday. You should let him choose between one thing and another.'

"But my father laughed. 'No,' he said, 'he'll have to think it up all by himself. . . . It's easy to choose, but to think of something all by yourself—'

"By night time I despaired. 'I know what I want,' I said, 'I want another day to think in.'

" 'Another day!' my father said. And he laughed, for he had seen all along how it would end. 'Another birthday!' And he looked at my mother. 'Could we stand to be so nice to him for another whole day?' And my mother said, 'I'd have to bake another cake, and he ate so much today.'

"But I cried, 'No, not a cake! Not anything but just another day!'

"'Just another day,' my father said and put his head between his hands. 'And pretend to everybody that we made a mistake about the day he was born!'

"'No, but just another day to have anything I want!'

"My father shook his head. 'But it all goes together.'

"But my mother pleaded for me. 'Give him another day.'

"And so they gave me another. But it wasn't the same. When I woke in the morning, I knew it wasn't the same, because the day was not my birthday, and I would never have the courage to ask for something glorious."

Tom paused, for the eyes of the child were looking into his own; they were taking too much, taking more than the story, living in the life of the boy Tom Beckett. Tom wondered all at once if he were speaking the truth. Am I telling it the way it was or the way it is now?

He closed his eyes against the face before him. When he opened them, they focused on the tiny arched doorway of the church. "I cried about it to Emma in the twilight. Emma was the girl who stayed with me sometimes. In those days I told her everything. But Emma was very practical and strangely lacking in sympathy. I remember her very words. 'Well, nobody but God can give you back a day you done spent.' That was what she said, and I knew she was right.

"But for a long time afterward I asked myself the question: If I could have it back, what is it I would ask for? Every time I had a birthday after that, I asked myself the question, though my father never gave me such a chance again. He was kind not to do it. And do you know, each time I thought I knew the answer. But it was always something different. Something different every year. Once it was a horse. Then a boat. Then

61

a trip. And later . . . much later, there was a lady I loved and she died . . . and she was what I wanted. But now I think . . . now I think if I could have her, I'd be too old for her to want me. If somehow she was older too . . . but we wouldn't be the same. . . . We'd be almost strangers—"

He paused and looked at the boy. "I'm telling you this to show you that what seems so important to you now will someday—" But Tom could not finish. It seemed to him suddenly that he had spoken to the boy out of weariness of flesh—"Vanity of vanities . . . all things pass away"—that it was not to be forgiven. He had spoken in the language that a boy could understand, but with the heart of a man who remembered only dimly what it was to be alive. How much have I forgotten? he wondered. And the face of the boy was before him. All the symbols of growth and greenness that had always belonged to him, that David had sung for him, were somehow gathered in the face of this child: the green bay tree, . . . the cedars of Lebanon, . . . the little hills that rejoice at the rain, . . . the valleys that stand so thick with corn that they laugh and sing. And the young eyes had taken each word that he had spoken and were holding them out for Tom Beckett to see.

"Timothy," he said at last, "we all have our troubles. I have locked mine up inside me, thinking, I suppose, that they were mine and I shouldn't bother other people with them, that I might make people a little less happy if I told them. But I think I was wrong. . . . When you lock away your troubles, you lock away a little of yourself. And after a while you may be all locked away. And God did not intend that. Not at all. Not at all. People should be free to come and look in your windows and ask you to come out and talk with them a little and maybe hear their troubles. If you are locked away with yours, you can never know theirs. And then you can never help . . . if you don't even know."

He could not say why, when the hand began to move beneath the cat's white throat, he felt it in himself as a kind of reproach. And again it seemed hard, as it had seemed the night before, that he was held accountable to God for every man that walks the earth. And every child.

"Right now, Timothy, you're one of my troubles, and I shall ask God to help me."

The boy watched him steadily, with the face on the slender neck that even yet could turn away. "I shall pray for you and for myself. And I shall keep on praying."

"Tonight?" asked the boy. It was the first word between them, and the voice struck a chord deep in Tom Beckett's heart, where he seemed to know the voice. It was so much a child's that, hearing it, he could not catch his breath for a moment. Nothing, he had come to know, is quite what we expect, and when it is, we feel the shock.

He waited before he spoke. "Tonight and every night. And every morning too. And in between times, I think."

The boy said slowly, "Do you ever pray for cats?"

There was a stillness in the room. Tom felt a flutter in his throat that was close to panic. He chose his words with care. "I believe I have not up to the present moment prayed for them." He felt as if he were embarking on an uncharted sea.

He waited, but nothing came. There was only the automatic purring of the cat, so faint he scarcely heard it. He said at last, "Is your . . . friend here in trouble?"

The boy gripped the head of the cat till she ducked and twitched her ears into shape.

"Was it something about her kittens?" Tom ventured at last. He saw that he was right. "And your aunt . . . she won't let you keep them?"

The boy's eyes were hard. "Last time . . . last time she murdered 'em." He sat rigid, pinioned, as if his knees still gripped the shoulder of the bell.

Tom looked away. "Yes," he said. "Yes, . . . yes." He was assenting to the tenseness, the rigidness before him, to the hiding in the tower, the altar hangings on the floor. To all of it suddenly, unreasonably, he assented.

He found that he did not want to think, but to sit there quietly with the boy before him. It was a little like the way he had felt a fortnight ago when he had done his Christmas shopping, such as it was; when having battled with the crowds, found nothing that he had in mind, and bought it anyway, he came home, sat down, decided it was finished and he would think no more about it.

He even felt remotely that the whole thing was humorous—humorous, with a touch of blasphemy somewhere about the edges. He felt no more inclined to smile at the humor than to disapprove of the blasphemy.

The afternoon was edging into paleness. The sun was slanting through the window and falling on the roof and tower of the tiny church before him. And slowly, subtly, as if it were an ache in his own tired breast, he grew aware of the trouble before him: not a child's trouble or even the trouble of another being than himself, but a trouble, . . . a pain. A crack in the universe. A flaw in the perfection, the rightness of things.

But nothing is right, he reminded himself in a kind of wonder. Nothing in this fallen old world can be right. Yet here before him was a deep expectation of rightness, a profound disappointment in the working-out of things. Not so much a rebellion against the wrongness—that perhaps would come later—as an expectation of the rightness.

And suddenly this seemed a fresh and wonderful thing. I have been too long away from children, Tom thought. And then it came into his mind, perhaps because of the season, that the child in the manger had been born with such an expectation of rightness in the world; and that somehow those who saw the Cross in Him, before He scarcely knew the world around Him, were wrong, all wrong. He had come into this world with faith and trust in the rightness. And even in His darkest hour, even in the Garden, there lay beneath His prayer the everlasting might-have-been, . . . the wondrous possibility that men will turn from their ways.

I must remember this, he thought. I must say it tomorrow night. And then he was ashamed to be thinking of his sermon before the boy.

In the face of all his past—the death of Katherine and the sterile years—there stirred in him now, faintly, that expectation. That ignorance, he might have called it. Or even that blindness. But he did not call it that.

He longed to tell the child he had been right: The world is lovely. Or was it that Tom wanted, after all these years, to know it? "Timothy," he said, "there are many things I can't begin to make right. But this is something I can help you with . . . if you will trust me."

And even as he said it, he was aware too keenly that he could not restore the vanished mother, . . . the vanished home, the love. He could do little more than reinstate a cat in someone's temporary graces.

He began to pace the floor as he did for sermon writing, as if the boy were not around.

The cat leaped to the floor and lay in wait to love him. She seemed to lavish most of her affection on his injured leg. With unerring instinct, she selected it.

He stopped in his pacing. "What do you call your friend?"

"Cornelia."

"Cornelia." He almost smiled. "You liked the name? Or you knew somebody named it?"

It was written in the boy's face that it had been his mother's name.

"Yes, . . . yes," said Tom Beckett said and turned away. Presently he asked, "She has been with you for some time?"

"Just about a year . . . no, . . . not that long. She came on my birthday. That was how I got to keep her."

"She was a present," Tom said.

"No, she wasn't any present. She just came. But I thought she was a present. That's why she let me keep her."

"Your aunt?"

The boy nodded. "Sometimes they just come," he said. "You know how it is."

Tom inclined his head.

"When they come, they don't ever leave," Timothy said slowly. Tom heard the note of triumph, the cry of faith in the voice. Others leave, but not this. Others leave. . . . He braced himself against another onslaught from the cat. Others leave. . . .

He sent the boy and the cat out to play in the snow that was left. And he tried to remember what it was that he had meant to do this day. There was a meeting at the City Hall. But he had long since missed the hour. And he had promised to attend the Christmas pageant at the Baptist church. He looked at the clock. He would miss that too. The Missionary Guild had been in session for an hour. He had been asked to say a word about the Congo, he recalled. He settled for calling the list of numbers on his desk.

When he finished, there was not a great deal left of the day: only a little silver in the air and on the walks, a little purple in the branches, and the church looming gray beyond the window—looming larger, as it did at every dusk, till it was the whole horizon.

He rang up an eating place around the corner that delivered. All they made were pizzas, and he had eaten them before. But having missed his lunch, he felt that he was

66

equal. He ordered two, deluxe. When they came, he called in the outcasts. He poured them milk in the kitchen, and there unveiled the pizzas. On second thought, remembering a sleepless night, he gave his portion to Cornelia. She ate the sausage first, and he had the impression that she had coped with one before.

Noting the rough and grimy hands, he was aware of some responsibility. He sent Timothy to wash them beneath the kitchen faucet and was astonished at the rivulets of dirty water coursing down the sink, and at the look of the dish towel he had found for the drying, and then at the hands that emerged from it unchanged, still rough and still begrimed.

Timothy glanced at his face. "That's just the way they look. All the time."

"I expect," said Tom gravely, "that we forget to sweep out the tower."

"That's just the way they look." He put them in his pockets. Then he granted, "It was pretty messy up there." He looked at Cornelia biting into a mushroom. "She was having to wash herself about all the time."

Tom had a fleeting vision of the altar cloths upon the floor. "It's because we hardly ever need to go up there," he said. "In fact we keep it locked. With a key." And he looked at the child suggestively, . . . a little sternly perhaps.

Timothy made no sign. But with a guarded air, he drew one hand from his pocket.

While the boy was eating, Tom secretly watched him, seeing how swiftly he came alive as he ate, came into a kind of power, till he seemed on the brink of being anything at all. Anything was possible; nothing was fixed. From moment to moment he was in the midst of growth. Tom was accustomed to summing up a thing. He liked to take a present face and file it neatly in the past. Watching this child, he seemed to swim against the tide.

He got up to stop the dripping of the water in the sink. "Did you have a nice time in the tower?" he asked, so elaborately casual that he amazed himself. Hand tense upon the faucet, he listened to the silence, and then to the answer.

"It's pretty high up."

"Yes, it is."

"You get to thinkin' you might fall."

"Yes, you do," said Tom.

And suddenly the words seemed to sum up his life, and the life of the child, and to bind the two together till he could not breathe.

He found that he was very tired but no longer hungry. He drew some water for the kettle and made a cup of tea. At his feet, Cornelia was attacking the cheese. When she had finished, she licked herself discreetly with a secret air, bathing each limb in turn, now tender, now detached. Her flexible pink tongue could take any shape at all, could be innocent or evil, like a bird's or like a snake's.

He reminded himself that she was one of God's creatures. And now, with her aura of motherhood, there was about her a quality, introspective, withdrawn. She gazed at him remotely with green, slanted eyes, and then slowly closed them, shutting him out. He began to find something quite fitting in her name. She had the regal air of that Roman matron who had brought out her sons and called them her jewels; she had been Cornelia too. And suddenly in her distant, staring eyes he saw himself reflected, a tiny point of a figure, infinitely small. . . .

His leg was aching. The strain of the day was upon him: the climb in the tower, the adapting to new things, and the strain—he acknowledged it—of being with the young, with Bill and with this child. It was as if inside him there was the constant whisper, "More . . . more. Wider . . . wider. Deeper . . . deeper"; yet he was never enough, never wide enough, or deep enough. He paced the kitchen while Timothy finished eating. And the two of them watched, in league and proof against him.

He put Timothy and Cornelia in the room where the bishop always stayed when he arrived. He laid some pajamas of his own on the high tester bed, then went away, and wandered from room to room, vaguely lost. He savored them, detached and faintly curious, as if they had been lived in by some one other than himself, some one slightly eccentric of whom he had not approved. Already the spirit of the child dispossessed him in his house. He found himself at last in his mother's room. He could not remember having been there since her death nearly four years ago. It was just as she had left it. But he felt himself a stranger. He could not quite recall the way she had looked, or her voice, or her walk, . . . or the love that was between them.

He returned to the bishop's room. Timothy was in bed. A small heap of clothes was on the floor beside it. The pajamas were still lying folded at the foot. Some feathers from the tower were lying on the pillow.

Without a word, Tom walked to the window that opened on the moonlit roof and locked it. He did not look at the boy; but with a kind of shame that was sharp and unexpected, he returned to the door. And he stood there, so conscious of his failure and of the gesture that had sealed it that he could not say good night. Something in him whispered that he had betrayed himself. Or was it God he had betrayed? For all at once the labor of his ministry had ended in this: that he should go to lock a window to prevent a child's escape.

"Did you want anything? More covers? A glass of milk?" They were the things he always asked the bishop, who always answered no. No one who had slept in this room had ever required anything of him at bedtime.

He switched out the light and was turning away, when

Timothy said suddenly, "Will you sit with me till I go to sleep?"

It was so unforeseen that Tom thought he had not heard it. He turned around slowly, a sharpness in his throat. They were the very words Katherine . . . the last words of all.

"With the light on?" asked the child.

Tom switched it on again, drew a chair to the bed, and sat down beside it.

Timothy's eyes were closed, the covers drawn to his chin, and under them, beside his shoulder, a rounded lump would be Cornelia. They seemed to him so slight, so lost, and so nameless, in the white expanse of bed.

"Till I go to sleep?" the boy asked.

"Till you go to sleep." He was trying to forget the pattern of the words—an ordinary pattern anyone could find. Of course it is the dark. I was afraid of it too. And all at once there was no longer any need to be wider and deeper; his presence was enough. It was enough that he should sit here, holding back the dark. He relaxed in the wonder of it. . . .

Thinking the boy asleep in the lighted stillness, Tom turned off the bed lamp. And when they were in darkness he could hear the faint purr of the cat beneath the covers. Then he knew that Timothy had opened his eyes, that they looked at one another, he and this child. Between them the dark was more alive than the light. He tried to say, "Close your eyes, go to sleep." But he did not want it to end. He could not explain it, but it was as if he sat by Katherine's bed for the last time and watched her life go out—as many times he had dreamed it—and here he was still sitting and her life was coming back.

He heard the even breath of the child above the purring. He leaned back and closed his eyes and prayed for the child and for himself. He recalled that he had been this very age, this child's age, when he had found his God. But no, there was a time before. . . . And then he was looking back to when it all began. . . .

The seed had lain in darkness until one day at twilight when he was three or four. They had all been staying at the little lodge in the woods where his father liked to hunt in the winter. There was a girl named Emma who came along to cook for them and to sit with him when his mother had to drive into town. She was a distant cousin of his father's who liked to earn the extra pay. Sometimes she read to him words from the Bible. She could not make a thing sound so well as his mother. Even a passage she had done before she read aloud in a halting, new voice, as if for the first time, the first in all the world. She was the only person in those early days who thought to let him hear what the Bible was like. She kept it hidden somewhere and brought it out and opened it, as if God had just revealed to her where He had placed it and she had looked and there it was. She read to him of Abraham and Isaac in her halting voice that discovered the words for the very first time. He trembled a little, though he did not at all understand what it meant: why Abraham was ready to kill his son. But it came so new in the mouth of Emma that it had no time to take on a meaning. It was there; it was all.

Later, much later, he thought it a pity that people should study the passage closely, to shake their heads or defend it stoutly. It should always be read in the voice of Emma before it ever had time to mean. It should lie, each word slowly, freshly spoken, at the bottom of the heart and be stamped with awe, and then sealed with faith. He believed it was written to be read so. As God said once to Abraham, "Take now thy son," perhaps He said now, "Read this," and you rose, like Abraham, without a word and read. . . . When you received the Scriptures so—as rarely now they were received—the slow, rich incense of the Lord enveloped and made sweet the words, and gave them more than meaning, . . . gave them power to hallow. So he believed.

It was Emma who had told him about the chair—a little chair, well but roughly made, that had belonged to his father when he was a child and was brought to the cabin for Tom to sit in. He had been fond of pushing it in front of the window, where he could stand and look out at the woods. Once when he had cried to play in the snow, Emma made him sit in it quite alone in the room. And when he got up and walked away, she put him sternly back and told him the chair had been made long ago in the carpenter's shop by Jesus Himself, the very Jesus who was nailed to the cross. "And look at you," she said, "you don't want to sit in it!"

He became very still until she left the room. Then he grew afraid and began to cry. Will I be nailed to a cross? he thought. But he was not sure that he knew what that meant, though Emma had one time explained it to him. He could not worry about it for long, because it began to grow dark in the room, and he was supposed to be afraid of the dark. He wondered if Emma would bring the light if he cried. He felt the chair, the arms and the back, and it seemed to him then that he liked the dark, with the light from outside coming in at the window over his head. Quite suddenly he stood on the seat of the chair. And in the twilight, beyond the glass, was the face of a deer looking in at him just above the sill. The woods behind it were caught in the night. Perhaps the deer had run away from the dark. For he saw that it was a child like himself. The snowflakes were pelting the brown, speckled back. It stood with its nose very close to the glass, its eyes glowing softly into his own. And then it turned and ran into the woods. He sat down again in the chair that was made for him long ago. Or it might have been just made for him, for indeed he had so little past of his own that he could not understand about the long ago. He sat still, loving the eyes of the deer and knowing they were made for him. And after a while Emma came in with the light, and it was made for him. . . .

Growing older, he understood that all the world was made for him. But he did not know what to do with this knowledge, until he saw that he in turn was made for all the world. He had it in his mind obscurely to give the world some glorious thing that would somehow prove the plan for him. And then one night, one Christmas Eve, he knew that God had made him for Himself.

They were sitting alone in the house in town, he and Emma. His mother and father had gone to church, and he was supposed to be in bed. Emma had come in from her home in the country to stay with him and to help with dinner on the following day. He was eight at the time, and he had not been allowed to go to midnight service. He did not mind, but neither did he care for the thought of Emma sitting up with him as if he were a child. To prove that he was not, he sat up with her. She did not protest, but dozed beside him, dreaming into the fire. And when it struck midnight, she looked around. "Think of it," she said. "At home all the animals are kneeling to God."

"What animals?" he asked. He was proud of being more awake than she.

"All the animals," she said. "All the cows and the horses. And the sheep. They saw Jesus first. Before even the shepherds."

He laughed because lately Emma seemed to him silly. "They have to kneel to lie down," he said. "That's the way they sleep."

But she shook her head, looking into the fire. "It's Christmas Eve. And many's the time I've gone out and seen 'em."

"Sure," he said. "It's the same every night. Only then you go to bed as soon as it's dark."

73

"It's not the same. It may look the same, . . . but that don't mean it's the same at all."

Soon after came the sound of the key in the latch. "Off to bed with you," she said, "or we'll both be in trouble."

Silently he had run up the stairs and leaped into bed with a singing in his heart. He would just close his eyes and then it would be morning. But before he shut them, he looked out of the window beside his pillow, and the moonlight was lying all over the ground. And beyond the fence, underneath the shed, his little horse was kneeling. He raised the window and whistled softly. Jim never stirred but went on kneeling. The moonlight seemed as warm as the fire on the hearth below, and the trees and the hedges and the roofs of the houses were being made new in the warm pale light that belonged to the earth before the first sunrise. He lowered the window and lay down and covered his head with the blankets. In the darkness God whispered, "I am making you new."

And then he was back in another dark, in the chair God had made for him long ago, and Emma was coming in with the light.

Now he was sitting beside this child. And the chair, this chair, might have been the same, so at peace he felt, so full of a power he had not known for years. He had found his God so young it was like opening his hand and there He was. Then it had been closed for him when Katherine died. God was left inside, but nothing else was there. Now it almost seemed as if it opened a very little and that everything he touched with it again must live.

He stood up quietly and left the room and went downstairs to his sermon for the morrow. For a while, as he paced, the words that would contain the joy of God's coming seemed to be at hand. But his leg began to ache from hunting them down . . . or from climbing in the tower. And the hickory nuts were hammering on the roof again.

Bill Ryder called up and asked permission to modernize the spelling of the passage by John Donne. He was doing the bulletin.

"I think not," Tom said, trying not to sound provoked. "I really don't see why. The spelling, I rather fancy, has a charm of its own."

"But I thought the impact might be greater—"

"Impact. . . . Impact! The sentiment is really of another age. It cannot be translated into ours, not entirely." Then he said—and he could hear the irritation in his voice—"Let the service be the impact." And then he hung up.

"Impact . . . ," he whispered. "That's a word the young ones use. Implying you should brace yourself to hear about God." Every word of every sermon must be so many hickory nuts beating down the roof.

All at once his heart and leg began to ache together, as they sometimes did, till he did not know the one from the other, and he almost called Bill Ryder back to tell him to spell it any way he pleased. But the florist rang up for permission to hammer seven nails above the door of the church. He had in mind some holly—

"Nails!" He raised his voice. He almost said that it was not the Crucifixion but the Birth. . . . Nails were quite impossible.

He hung up humbly. After years of such requests he had fallen out of charity with every florist in town.

He locked the door at last and turned down the heat a bit and went upstairs to bed. He looked in upon the sleeping boy as he passed. Cornelia was lying on top of the covers; her eyes were green fires in the darkness of the room.

He turned away, as if she had forbidden him to walk in and recapture anything again. He went into his room and began to undress.

Thinking of the phone calls, he was sick at heart. Not because he had allowed himself to be provoked, but because—and this was where, all unexpectedly, his guilt seemed to lie—they had not really mattered. Nothing really mattered, nothing in this world. But for too long he had pretended that it did. . . .

My crying sins . . . and my whispering sins.

It was his secret that he held this life of small account. And secret was the way in which he dealt with it, not quite engaging himself or, at any rate, the best of himself, of his mind and his heart. He struck it a glancing blow in passing and allowed it to strike him a like one in return—a sporting gesture. Yet he was conscious that an air of detachment would not do for the ministry. And so all too often he affected an impatience, a testiness, a gruffness, as if he were quite at home with life and felt its pricks to excess and was moved to grumble like the rest of them. Impatience, after all, is but a way of saying that life has better things in store. He persuaded the others that it did, he trusted. Sometimes, almost, he persuaded himself.

He was aware that with his curate he was most in danger of being discovered, and therefore, he was gruffest with Bill. To his curate, he complained of all the things that in the depths of his heart did not concern him. Still, at times he caught a puzzled look in Bill Ryder's eyes, as if he hovered on the brink of understanding. There was something in Bill's eyes that was almost love—not Christian love, not *agape,* but that other love more disturbing to the older man, the love of son for father. And when he saw it there, he wanted to go down on his knees to Bill Ryder and ask his forgiveness. Instead, he always found a way of sending the younger man about his business.

Now, sighing deeply, he turned out the light and knelt beside his bed, with the tower in the window. "Let the tower with all its bells fall on thee . . . retreat thee into thy nothingness." He was quiet for a while, and it seemed to him the tower lay upon him and each of its bells struck him

76

deeper in his soul, till down where he was nothing, not an echo could be heard. He struggled into being. In the darkness he remembered how John Donne had said it: "If there were any other way to be saved and to get to Heaven, than by being born into this life, I would not wish to have come into this world. . . ."

But even as he embraced the words, the sleeping presence of the child lay upon him, covered him with an indescribable longing, as if there were a fullness, here, now, a sweet wholeness that had always been his own; he had only to reach out and draw it into himself. The effort not to reach was almost more than he could bear. And yet how could it be there? It is my time of life, he reasoned. The flesh is never laid to rest with promises of Glory. It will never understand how empty is the world. It is always crying out for something this side of Heaven. And when the end of life approaches, it only cries the more, saying, "Mark the little time. . . ." And slowly he prayed for himself and for the child and for all who after this night would minister to the child. He prayed the other things he always prayed; and he stood up and walked around the room a bit to limber up his knee for the night. Then he got into bed.

But when he lay beneath the tower, he could not be at rest. At last, turning on his back with his eyes on the bell room, he prayed another thing: "In so far as animals are of concern to Thee and may be prayed for—" But he could not finish.

In the house the child's sleep lay as heavy as incense.

He was dreaming in the night that Timothy had opened the window of his bedroom and climbed out upon the roof. In the moonlight, he was running down the slope of it, and then he was falling. . . .

But it was Tom Beckett falling down the tower into sleep.

When Tom rose in the morning, his knee began to warn him of unpleasantness ahead; so while he ate the soft-boiled egg prepared by Mrs. Travis, he was bracing himself. In the face of premonition, he retreated to his study and completed his Comment for the service that night. He read it over quickly with a sinking heart, trying to imagine the sound of it when spoken in the midst of all the glory of the midnight hour.

He was almost relieved when at nine o'clock it broke. The Chairman of the Altar Guild was ringing his doorbell. He saw from her face that it was she that was decreed for him. But he found that, though he could not guess her mission, he was indeed well braced.

"Mrs. Culpepper," he said in a holiday voice, as if he had anticipated her with special pleasure.

"May I speak to you a moment?"

"Yes, indeed. Come in." And he stood aside, allowing her to precede him to the study. Marching behind her, he paid tribute to the terrible consistency he had observed in her nature. The fact that she wore the same hat in every season was little more than symbolic of the fact that she wore the same face in every season. Yet he fancied that through the years—and there had been so many—he had become proficient in reading her subtle variations of expression. In the lines of her face dire events of one degree or another were everlastingly proclaimed. Sometimes it was nothing more than the failure of the candles on the altar to be dripless. Today it would appear that she had just witnessed the Battle of Armageddon; it had not gone as foretold.

She sat in the chair he offered her, but at once she rose again. "Mr. Beckett," she began, "a terrible thing has happened—"

He knew her thirst for drama. For a full moment, before replying, he joined her forces; he looked deeply concerned. "My dear lady," he said at last. He had always been grateful that his had been the era when "my dear lady" could be inserted into any situation, so that coming from his lips it sounded quite at home. There was no modern interjection that could indicate so much . . . so much chivalrous respect that committed one to little, so much marking of time that did not suggest retreat. He offered it again: "My dear lady—"

"Mr. Beckett," she took the plunge with professional sense of timing, "the linens and the hangings for the altar for tonight are missing from the sacristy! They have recently been taken, because we checked three days ago. The white hangings were checked and put back on the shelf. The linens were laundered. And now the Fair Linens—the three of them—are gone. And the Christmas hangings—the white Superfrontal has been taken from the shelf. And the red one. And the green one as well."

Plainly, her words suggested, the church was out of business for several seasons to come. She looked at him, her features charged with solid disaster. He felt a little quiver at the base of his stomach, an uneasy feeling that she had come into her own and intended to stay. "We have found a Corporal missing."

He cleared his throat. "Only one Corporal?" He saw at once that it was not the thing he should have said.

"Some one has made a clean sweep!" she finished.

"Do sit down, Mrs. Culpepper."

"I cannot sit," she announced. Indeed, she seemed to be saying that she would never sit again.

He turned from her and paced up and down the rug. He could have told her that he had observed a Purificator on the floor of the clock room. "Mrs. Culpepper," he said gently at last, "the son of God is about to be born again in the stable. And here we are getting out of sorts about the linens." He could tell from her quietly astonished face that he had just said something quite unlike himself.

"We have always tried," she said in a dedicated voice, her forces strengthened. "We have followed your own instructions to the letter." He had long ago observed that besides the royal "we" and the editorial "we," there is an altar guild "we."

"Yes," he said, "you have been most faithful and devoted."

"We have tried to be," she said. And in her eyes was the question: What more is required of us?

He wanted to answer her: "A sense of proportion." But then he would be lacking in charity if he voiced it. A sense of proportion is almost never given to the dedicated. And dedication surely is the better thing.

"My dear lady," he said, "if you will sit here patiently, I shall undertake to find these linens . . . and the hangings."

"But how?"

"Have faith in me, Mrs. Culpepper!" he all but thundered.

He did not look at her face, but he went out quickly and shut the door and stood in the living room, ashamed of himself. Then he pulled himself together and walked upstairs, short of breath.

Timothy was lying on his stomach on the bed. Cornelia lay beside him.

"Timothy," he said, "a crisis has arisen." He swallowed and revised it. "What I mean is this: The altar linens and the hangings, the things you were making your bed with in the tower—," he flinched a little when he said it, "—they have got to be brought down. In a hurry, you understand. Now, the thing is this: My leg, you see, it's not much good for climbing; so what I want you to do is to run back up and get these things together in a very neat bundle—so they won't drag, you know, and get all dirtied up in coming down the steps. You understand?"

The boy nodded and got up from the bed.

"These things, you know, belong on God's altar. . . . You understand what the altar is, don't you?" he said.

The boy nodded again. And it seemed to Tom, looking into his face, that he knew and understood far better than most, and that he was not afraid . . . and that it would be wrong to drop the guilt of desecration into his soul.

"Do you still have the key to the tower?" Tom asked, afraid for a moment that Bill might have got it. The boy touched the pocket of his pants and smiled. "And Timothy," he added, "don't go out the front door. Go out the kitchen door. Very quietly, you know: And come back the same way." He was ashamed to be saying it, but his spirit was craving peace. All needless explanations to the lady who awaited he desired to spare himself.

With a kind of resignation, he watched the cat leap past him to follow the child. If she decides to have another go at the birds in the bell room and remains overlong and has these kittens in the tower—. He would not finish the thought.

He waited, pacing back and forth from bed to dresser, pausing to ruffle pages of the guest book on the table containing signatures of persons, some more, some less august: Reverends, Right Reverends, Very Reverends, . . . and a deacon or two.

He was pulling out his watch when he heard the footsteps on the stairway, and in a moment the altar hangings and the linens were in his arms. They were indeed a little rumpled, but he shook them out with a cursory sort of reverence and descended to the study.

Mrs. Culpepper stared at the burden in his arms and seemed unable to speak.

"Well," he said with dignity, "you see I have them here."

"Mr. Beckett," she pronounced.

He could not tell if she accused him or if she spoke his name to be assured that it was truly he who proffered her these desecrated things. He was careful not to follow her gaze to the linens.

"How are we to manage? The service is tonight. The lady who takes care of all our things for the altar—I doubt she's available on Christmas Eve—"

"Mrs. Travis," he interrupted, "is excellent with an iron. She will turn these out in no time."

She looked at him in silence. "Mrs. Travis is not a member," she stated at length.

"A member of the Altar Guild? Or a member of this congregation?" He tried to calm himself. "She is neither, I

83

grant you. But she is a member of God's family. I have baptized her with my own hand—" He strode a few paces away and returned. "I shall stand for Mrs. Travis that she will wash and iron these with reverence."

Mrs. Culpepper drew her lips together.

What more? he thought, his pressure mounting. Should I grant her absolution while the iron heats?

When at last she had departed, he took a little tablet from his desk and drank it down with water, to steady him a little. This is bad for me, he thought, brooding over the kitchen sink. This is very, very bad for the body and the spirit. I should retire. . . . But he knew he did not mean it. He always said it as a penance when he tangled with the guilds.

He loosened his collar and sipped his water slowly. Then he went upstairs.

Timothy was lying on his stomach again. "Timothy," he said, "don't take the altar linens . . . if you should do this again."

The boy nodded gravely. And it was laid to rest between them.

Tom sat on the bed. Cornelia was lying on the open guest book on the table. He could see that she was all but covering a bit of poesy that a bishop had composed upon a visitation. When you became a bishop, he reflected, you were lost to ordinary shames. He felt again at peace. "This bed is rather good for sleeping, don't you think? Much better than the tower, I would say, wouldn't you?"

"Better than my bed at home," Timothy agreed. "I sleep with my cousin and he kicks all night."

"Does he, now? Does he, now?"

"All night long."

And suddenly it was like a hand upon Tom Beckett's throat that tonight the boy would be gone from this house.

But God will be left. The way he was left after Katherine

84

died. He thought it slowly, tensely, gripping the bedpost. He remembered then to say: Katherine died, and there isn't any more. There can't be any more. . . . And he saw all at once how his loss had grown bloodless, had grown into words. He had kept the lack of wife and children carefully at bay, fashioned it into a formless longing he could grow old with. And now this child appeared to give the longing flesh.

It shakes the heart to look into the face of what you seek. And he rose with an effort and went to the window.

"You think it might be time to eat pretty soon?" this child asked.

"Not yet, I shouldn't think."

His soul cried out against it; this should be a time of laying things to rest, a time of calmness after storm. But deep inside him was the knowledge that he had never known the storm. He had found his God so young it was like opening his hand. . . . Even the loss of his beloved had been a quiet, slow withdrawal. It seemed to him that he had dreamed one night that she was gone, and when he woke the dream was real. He had seen it as the grace of God that this was so. There had been no sons to give up to this world or the next. This too, he used to tell himself, could be God's grace.

And yet . . . and yet perhaps all men must know the storm at last. If not sooner, then later. If not without, then within. If not to lose your own son, then another's.

But this is sheer, sheer folly, he protested. I never saw this child before. I may never see him again.

He waited until he knew that his voice could be trusted. "Will you be glad to be going home again?" He saw the boy's face in the mirror turn to him.

"No," Timothy said. "I don't like my aunt."

"You like your cousins a little?"

"Not very much."

85

Tom closed his eyes. "You must come back and visit me again sometime."

The boy did not reply.

"Down here, you know. Not up there."

At last he said, "Have you forgiven me for keeping you last night?" He listened to the silence of the child, to the gentle, automatic purring of Cornelia. "Well," he said, "we won't press it."

He walked to the door. "If you're really very hungry, we'll ask Mrs. Travis for something." And he turned and looked at Timothy, as if he would remember how he lay in this room. Come, now, he told himself. Come, now. Come, now. You're too old for this. And there's work to be done. . . .

In the kitchen, Mrs. Travis was making something in a bowl, which mysteriously she covered with a towel at their approach. She turned on them a little wildly, sleeves unbuttoned but unrolled, hair wisping, a spot of flour in the corner of her mouth.

"What is it, Reverend?"

She did not like to be invaded in the midst of her duties. It was understood that in the mornings the Reverend kept to his study. Baptism had unstrung her nerves, she sometimes confided. Tom had tried, but he had failed to understand. Possibly she struggled with a sense of sin. He wondered uneasily if his instruction had been clear.

Now conscious of her post-baptismal state, for which he dimly felt accountable, Tom encroached upon her with a humble face. Since Mrs. Culpepper's retreat he was thrust into a vague accountability for all the ills of the world. "Hunger has come upon him all at once," he explained.

Good humor suddenly struck her. He had noticed that the Christmas season inclined to make her variable and to make her humors more pronounced. When she was gay at Christmas, she could be whimsical, hilarious. When she was depressed, she could be morbid, macabre, even. And sometimes, on occasion, these extremes were rashly mingled, such as on a Christmas Eve when the tensions took their toll.

"Well, of course it has. It's ten o'clock." And she produced an apple from the pantry and washed it in the sink. "They're full of arsenic," she said. "You got to be very careful." She patted Timothy on the head with a floury hand. "They say you keep all the arsenic you ever ate inside you and you keep on adding to it, and finally you get enough, till one more little bit, like one more little apple you don't bother to wash—"

It reminded Tom of the way that Emma used to talk about the road to Hell: a little sin every day, and then one more tiny lie, no blacker than the rest—one more stolen teacake, however stale it be—and you were done for. He said, with his eyes on the head of the child, "I thought an apple a day kept the doctor away."

"But not the undertaker."

"I see, . . . I see."

"My," she said to Timothy, "and you'll be going home today." She disappeared onto the back porch and returned in triumph with a jacket from the box for missions in the basement of the church. "I'd rather it went to him than to the heathen," she announced.

"I'm sure," said Tom, "that Timothy has a jacket of some sort at home. But we will borrow it for the occasion. And thank you, Mrs. Travis. . . . But look both ways when you return it. I cannot have you getting into trouble with the guilds." He paused and fixed her with his eye. "You are suspected," he said mildly, "of borrowing coffee for my breakfast from the basement kitchen to save a trip to the store."

"Never!" she said stoutly. "Not since I was baptized."

Timothy retreated to the doorway to balance the apple on his tongue.

"Mrs. Travis," said Tom, mentally girding his loins for the fray, "there is a bundle of linens on the chair in my study. They belong on the altar for the service tonight. They must be washed and ironed before you leave this afternoon. The heavy thing of silk—just the white one is needed—perhaps it can be sponged. . . . You will know, I am sure, exactly what is required. They must be clean, you understand." Again he fixed her with his eye. "Clean enough for God." He knew the words to be unfair, and he spoke them with regret.

"Clean enough for God?"

"Clean enough for God."

"Oh, Lord," she said, "you never know in this house. When I took this situation it looked like nothin' at all."

"I know," he said. "I know."

"The bishop and the other reverends comin' to be fed—"

"Sometimes," he acknowledged, "I forget to let you know."

"There was another situation I could've had at the time. With a couple that worked, and them gone all day."

He cleared his throat. "I have always felt," and he examined his heart before he said it, "that Divine Providence guided you."

"I would-a taken it," she stated, "but I had it in the back of my mind to be saved."

"Yes." He nodded gravely. "And I have always counted it my privilege that you came to me for baptism."

She said, "It don't make me feel as settled as it should."

"I doubt if most of us will feel entirely settled till we find ourselves in Heaven."

Timothy was feeding a bite of apple to the cat.

"I wonder," she said, "if soup for lunch would be enough."

"Quite enough, Mrs. Travis."

"And no supper in the warmer?"

"No supper in the warmer."

She said, "I had a feelin' when I woke up. Like it was the bishop or some other reverend comin' to be fed."

"And now, if you'll excuse me, I'll get out of your way."

He retreated with relief and went in search of Bill Ryder in the basement of the church. He found him in his office at the end of the hall, smelling freshly shaven in the small, airless room.

"This is a miracle," he stated. "I find you without the customary search." He was fleetingly annoyed that Bill was so infrequent with the cropping of his hair. He had lately suspected that Bill trimmed it himself. If he would take a little more off the sides . . .

"In another minute I'd been gone."

"I wonder," said Tom, gazing absently at the outsize photograph of a girl upon the desk, "if it would take up too much time to make a note of where you're off to and leave it on the desk."

"You mean now?" asked Bill.

"No, no, no, . . . I mean at other times. Sometimes, you know, I need you."

"You need me now?"

"No, . . . no. But sometimes, you know, I like to talk things over." He sighed and looked around the little room, at the green metal files against the wall and the Church School leaflets stacked in the corners. Secretly, there were times when Tom wished his curate were not so easily pleased with circumstances or with his senior's importunities. It seemed to show evasion. At any rate, Tom found himself resentful, when he said his prayers, that he must call himself to wonder if he should ask forgiveness for some unreasonable demand to which he had been tempted by Bill's amiable manner.

89

"The boy is still at the rectory. I take him home this afternoon."

"I can do it after five."

"No, . . . no. I plan to do it."

"Did you discover why he ran away?"

Tom propped himself against the desk. He brushed his hand across the keys of the typewriter. "I have no idea why he ran away. He has some sort of notion his cat wasn't wanted. Or the kittens weren't wanted. She's expectant, you know."

"I know," said Bill. And he ventured mildly, "Possibly he identifies himself with this cat."

"Is that what they give you in the seminary now? You make the whole thing sound pagan. He felt they were all in league to murder these cats since they murdered the last ones."

Bill shuddered. "Is it murder . . . with cats?"

"The Egyptians found it worse. They found it blasphemy." He began to pace the concrete floor, as far as he was able in the less than ample space. "He must be taught to love people. . . . He doesn't like people. He just likes this cat. . . . Why hasn't Miss Honicutt taught him to like people? She has failed him miserably." He saw that Bill watched him with the little grin he always wore when Tom was like this.

Tom took a turn about the narrow office and thumped the wall beside him. "Is this the best we can do for you?" he asked.

"This? It's big enough. I'm not around here much."

"Tell me," Tom said and turned to him, "this boy—this child—how is it we know nothing of him if he's one of ours? Nothing of his home, his life? How is it he was nothing but a name upon our rolls? How is it we never knew he lost a mother? This concerns me."

Bill looked at him with suddenly sobered eyes. "It concerns me too."

"It is a fact that we, and not Miss Honicutt, have failed him."

Bill swallowed sharply. "What you mean," he said at last, "is that I've failed him."

"We work together—"

"But the keeping up with all these people's lives is mine. You mean that."

There was a silence between them.

"I wouldn't like to put it in that way," Tom said and turned away. After a moment he began, "If the load is too much for you, I can begin again. I can take on as much of the calling as you say."

"There are people on the rolls I never see," Bill said at last, his voice constrained. "Maybe every six months. Maybe once a year. Maybe never."

"That isn't good."

"It's rotten."

Tom turned back to him. "Then I'll begin again."

His curate stared at him with eyes that held tears. "Forgive me," he said, "but I have to say it out—"

Tom tensed a little. "Say what, Bill?"

"Say it the way I see it. . . . The way I see it is this. . . . Keeping up with all these people and their lives . . . it isn't something you graduate from, is it?"

Tom made no sign.

Bill went on. "If it is, I don't want it. I don't want to graduate."

Tom Beckett said sadly, "You have seen me like this?"

"I've seen you as a wonderful man and priest."

"But not very helpful. I see, . . . I see."

"No, it isn't that at all. It's that I'd think you'd want to have a little of it back. As much as you could handle." He paused and looked away. "I keep thinking of what some guy who lectured one time at the seminary said: You've got to have it

91

whole. The whole life. The whole ministry. You can't climb up the holy mountain and not ever come back down."

"If you do, . . . what then?"

"I don't know what then."

"I see, . . . I see." Tom turned and walked away, as far as he was able in the narrow room. When he spoke again, his voice was low. "And you are thinking that you too would like to have it whole. The whole thing. The whole ministry. To give a sermon now and then. And to celebrate Communion . . . once a month, perhaps."

Bill did not speak. At last he said, "I'm thinking . . . why has it got to be divided up . . . the way it is? Wouldn't it be better if we each had it whole?"

Tom looked at him. "I must think," he said, and rubbed his hand across his face. He was suddenly very tired, and his knee was aching. "Where is it that she lives?" he asked. "I've lost the address." And seeing the puzzled look on Bill's face, "This woman. This aunt he lives with."

"I have it here." Bill turned to a green filing cabinet by the wall. "Here it is. Mrs. Davis . . . on Maple. It's not too far away. It's 403." He turned to his senior. "I can go—" Then he stopped. "Forgive me, Tom," he said.

"Of course I forgive you." The voice was carefully controlled. "What do I have you for if it's not to keep me in line?"

"I never meant it that way."

"Of course you did, but I can take it. Though I'm not sure you're right. Possibly adding another curate is the answer. But there's always the budget." He turned away to the door, but then turned back. "Would your having it whole . . . would it include the Altar Guild?" He paused very briefly. "I thought not," he said. He studied the floor. "But work me into the line of scrimmage. Across the street, you know. I really think the B team. If it's the one that plays on Thursdays."

He walked out of the narrow office and down the corridor.

He opened the glass-paned door and closed it carefully behind him and took the basement steps. The sun had climbed high. He pulled out his watch, and it was all of ten o'clock. Staring at the tiny second hand as it circled, he told himself again: When the time comes . . . when the time comes, I won't ask him to stay. And behind that tiny hand he saw for a moment an infinity of shrinking hands, each one smaller, but ever circling the point where he stood.

He got into his car and drove the distance to Maple Street. Deliberately, he studied the decorated, tinseled doorways, the shrubbery hung with bulbs, the cardboard sleighs and reindeer strung out across the lawns—all of it looking counterfeit and foolish in the sunlight. He did not think of Bill, of how he looked or how he spoke. He tried to think of how it was before he came, and how it would be when he left . . . and nothing in between.

The number 403 was so far back from the street, hidden in among the houses, that he all but missed it. Going up the walk, he recalled a little prayer he used to say before he rang a doorbell that was strange to him. Then, the burden of it lay beyond himself. Or he had used to feel it so.

She answered the doorbell herself, a pale-looking woman, young, with colorless hair. She knew him at once, before he told her. Her eyes went searching for the child, and he saw the vivid look in them, half stricken, half detached, that said almost aloud: So he has run away from you. . . .

"Mrs. Davis," he told her quickly, "I have the boy at my house."

She looked at him mutely.

"I thought it might be better if we had a little talk before I brought him home," he said.

She held the door open. "Come in." Her voice was scarcely audible.

He observed the room he entered. It was poorly furnished.

93

"May I sit here?" he asked, and he dropped into a chair more substantial than the rest. He looked closely at her face and could not remember having seen it before, except that he had reached the age when every face he saw seemed vaguely familiar and reminded him a little of some other face. He did not like to ask her if she ever came to church.

At last he said, "We haven't seen you in some time."

"I pick up the children every Sunday," she stated.

"Yes, . . . yes. Of course."

And then he observed that her eyes were full of tears. "Now, how many are there? How many children?" he asked.

"Four."

"Four, counting your sister's child?"

She nodded.

"I see. . . . And your husband—"

"He died two years ago."

"Yes, . . . yes. I see."

In her eyes the tears continued to well, but her voice was unmoved, as if she was used to them and scarcely knew they were there. But he heard the faint, bewildered echo of her words that filled the room: They all run away. . . . She moved her lips, and with a little shock he recognized the strange, blind thirst, the wildness of desire to run from all the others before they ran from her. He looked away quickly; and when he turned back, it was gone, that old desire he could not face in another . . . because it always struck the echo he must stifle in himself.

He was able to say, "It has been difficult to manage since then, I suppose."

The tears spilled out upon her face. As if she found the knowledge of them in his eyes, she raised her hand slowly to brush them aside. He braced himself against her tears, but he could not look away. They continued to form. "Please don't," he said at last, and was ashamed of having spoken it.

"I'm not crying." Her voice was still unmoved, and she looked at him with what he thought was pity. "This isn't crying."

The words somehow shocked him. They seemed to accuse him, to say that he had lost touch, . . . lost understanding of what was real and what was not, of what was grief and what was not.

"What is it, then?" he asked.

She watched him, her face expressionless. "I'm tired." She studied him for a long moment. "Have you ever been tired?"

He found that he could answer, "Yes, I have."

"I'm twenty-nine," she stated. "Were you tired then?"

He drew in his breath. The very age. The very age. It sounded deep inside him, as if a hand had struck a bell in that remote interior tower where he lived out his life.

After a while he nodded, then sat on in silence. There seemed nothing else to say. A clock was ticking somewhere in another room. From up the stairs, a child began to cry. He could see the way she listened, as if she took the cry into herself, until it seemed to come from her, from her face, from her eyes. But she made no move.

He rose. He plunged into the words that always marked his failure. "Mrs. Davis, . . . I have a little fund the church provides me for doing the things I may find that need doing. It is strictly my own affair—"

But he did not finish. When she looked away, he said, "I shall drop in on you again and perhaps we can talk."

She stood up too.

"There is another thing," he said, in a voice not his own but one that seemed to belong to very old age. "I hope you'll understand I'm not trying to interfere. . . . The child, . . . Timothy, . . . has a cat of whom he seems very fond." She looked past him at the door through which he presently

95

would walk. "About the kittens, . . . I wonder, . . . as a favor to me—"

"He can keep them," she said, the tears again in her eyes.

"Thank you, Mrs. Davis. I'll bring him back this afternoon."

She drew her eyes to his, the tears brimming over.

"You want him back?" He asked it, not knowing what he wanted to hear. A wild kind of longing held his breath in his throat, such a thing as he had never known before in his life.

"Oh, yes," she said. "I want him back very much."

And when he had the answer, he could not tell if he wanted it.

"I tried." She was looking straight into his eyes through her tears. "But I'll try again."

"I know that," he said. And there was nothing more to say.

He could tell that she was watching from the window as he walked away. And he seemed again to pace beyond the tiny window in his study. The sun was overhead. He made no shadow on the earth. . . .

When he was home, he did not go into the rectory, but entered the church by the transept and stood for some moments in the center aisle. Then he turned and knelt in one of the pews. Quite deliberately, he did not say to God any of the things he had grown accustomed to saying. "Yes, . . . yes," he finally whispered deep inside himself.

His eyes were on the shadowed roof above him, and a fragment of an ancient prayer of Evensong drifted into his mind. In the thirteenth century, when the matter of the vaulting was but poorly understood, many church vaults had collapsed soon after they were built. "Deare Lord," they prayed at evening, "support our roof this night, that it may in no wyse fall upon us and styfle us. Amen." He closed his eyes suddenly and held them closed in darkness, without thought, without prayer. . . .

. . . Then Bill Ryder was asking, "Didn't you ever want to run away? Did you do it?" . . . "No, I didn't."

But I did, he thought. When I was coming down the ladder, I ran away. And I never went home.

He opened his eyes slowly. The afternoon sun pouring through the windows fell on the rug before him in front of the chancel. It seemed the very sun, the very hour, he had waked to in the clock room so many years ago to find that he had fallen in descending the tower. "Yes, . . . yes," he thought again. And he knew that ever since that hour he had somehow gone astray in God's sight. How has it happened? How has it happened? He stared at the altar, then closed his eyes against it. I have found it too good. No, not too good, but I have found it the only good. I have loved God indeed, but not His creation.

Then a fear fell upon him in thinking of the many he might have led astray . . . and might yet lead astray, since of himself he possessed not the power to love. Give me love, he prayed. Give me love for the things You have made with Your hands and Your breath. Show me the goodness You have found in them Yourself. . . .

He walked to Bill Ryder's office and stood in the doorway, looking down at his young curate where he sat at his desk.

Bill stood up. "Come in."

Tom smiled slowly. "The second miracle today." He looked around the room. "I find you when I need you."

Bill Ryder waited.

"Were you busy?" asked Tom.

"Not too busy for you."

There was a small constraint between them, born of the morning's talk; and yet there was a seeking, a searching out, as if again they met, but not quite, and now could no longer accept it in this way.

"Well," said Tom at last, "I made it over there, you know."
Bill waited again.

"Frankly, I say this frankly, I wished for you along, . . .
Bill," he said. "I see the writing on the wall—" He turned
away. "When the time comes . . . when you leave here—" He
cleared his throat. "I've told myself I wouldn't ask you to
stay. And I won't." He picked up the program for the
evening's service and walked the length of the room with it
and back. "But the way it has come about, I can't do it any
more, the way it should be done, . . . the work you do.
There's something I've lost. Down in here, you know," and he
struck his chest and turned away. "Before you can talk to
them, you've got to believe in the worth of this life. And I
can't. I can't. God should be enough. And He is for me. But
somehow when I talk to them, He isn't enough, . . . I don't
understand it, but He isn't enough."

He creased the program slowly and put it in his pocket. "I
can give them words, you know. But it isn't words they want.
They want to feel something in me, . . . something that gives
them heart for the struggle." He turned to his curate. "Bill, I
haven't got the heart. I haven't had it for years. I've tried to
think it didn't matter in the work I had to do. But it does. I
know it now. They need what you've got." He studied the face
before him, faintly curious, detached. He looked away. "I'd
like to believe I need it too . . . what you've got. But I think
it's too late. You reach an age, you know, when it's hard to
turn around." He smiled, a little wryness at the corner of his
mouth. "I just had a birthday. Two days ago," he said.

Bill's voice was low. "It's not too late to celebrate, I bet."

"Yes, it is. It's too late."

There was a pause between them, self-conscious, half
alarmed. Tom straightened his shoulders slowly and kicked
out his knee. "Well, enough for confession. I've got it off my

mind. And now forget what I said. I don't want to have to see it in your face every day."

"I'm forgetting it," Bill said.

"That's good. Now, where were we?" He flung his knee again. "Oh, yes," he said. "I'm concerned about this little woman, Mrs. Davis. Her husband died two years ago. She's only twenty-nine. It isn't so much money, you understand. I find her attractive. And something about her indicates that she would be an interesting companion."

He stopped at the look on the other's face and reddened with impatience. "Bill," he said loudly, "I'm thinking of you! I'm too old for that sort of thing, and you know it."

The young man smiled at him with sweetness and charm, and went on smiling.

"Well, what is it?" Tom asked.

"You keep forgetting," Bill said, "that I'm engaged to be married." He cleared his throat and looked down at the floor. "On the other hand, now that you bring it up, you yourself—"

"Shut up, Bill!" said Tom. "I can read what you're thinking, and I don't like what I read." And after a brooding moment he began, "If you're suggesting that my Christian duty is to marry every unprovided-for woman of the parish—"

"The canons of the Church," Bill observed, "and the law of the land—"

"I know," said Tom. "I know, I know," as if the humor wearied him. "Bill," he said thoughtfully, "sometimes I address you . . . well, it may seem to you, rudely. . . . When I say, 'Shut up,' I don't mean quite that. Not at all, you know. You understand what I mean?"

"You mean you want me to sign off in a hurry."

"Exactly. . . . But yet not exactly that, either. . . . I think perhaps it's a term of affection."

Bill was looking at the floor intently.

"If I didn't like you, I couldn't indulge myself, you know."

"I'm honored," said Bill.

"Shut up," said Tom, and he walked out the door. At the end of the hall, through the glass of the door, he could see the sunlight falling down the basement steps. And he knew he had not finished.

He went back inside. "Bill," he said, "I'm asking you to take the service tonight."

The clock in the tower began to strike into their silence.

"There's nothing wrong with my health," Tom said crisply.

Bill Ryder did not speak, but there were tears in his eyes.

"And I'm not all that fond of you," Tom corrected him. "I need to say this to someone, and it might as well be you." He drew the evening program from his pocket and creased it once again and put it back. "I don't mind telling you it's a kind of penance. It seems to me I've been a little out of focus—" But after all he could not put it into words.

"You'll give the sermon?" Bill finally asked.

"No, I'll not be here." He ruffled the stack of programs on the desk with his thumb. "You have time enough, don't you? You probably have one prepared . . . in case this should happen . . . any old year. . . . I should have given you more notice. Except that I didn't know it myself, you understand."

Suddenly, without intending it, Tom met his curate's eyes, and it was deeply in them: the glance he could not meet— long formless, now forming; the glance of the son who seemed to know his father; the glance that would commit them both to this life, to this moment, to the terrible bond of love between the life and the moment. He almost said into it, "Don't leave me, Bill." But he turned away, shaken, saying instead, "Witherspoon, you know, will be glad to assist you. He's tired of retirement and offers me his services on the average of once a month."

He walked out the door, but turned once again. "Bill," he said humbly, standing in the hall, "if you would think about a

100

haircut. For tonight, you know." He watched his curate sweep his hand across his head.

"I guess I plain forget."

"I'll remind you . . . now and then." They looked at one another. Across the threshold, long and deeply, they met at last. "I still like to think we work together, you and I."

He glanced off down the hall and back again. "I hope," he said gravely, "that you have never taken offense at any thing I've said."

"I never have. I never will." Bill's voice was low. "But how could I? You never seem to live quite on a plane with the rest of us."

"No," Tom said, "I haven't."

"I mean that as a good thing—"

Tom waved this last aside and walked off down the hall. For the first time in his life, he asked himself the question: What shall I become? He had seemed to find the answer long ago, so long ago he could not remember having ever known the question. In that moment, it struck him as a bitter thing to have found the answer first. For now, in the midst of life, the question had appeared.

Climbing the basement steps, he was conscious that he had not eaten lunch. The soup would be cold, and Mrs. Travis would be wrestling with the linens for the altar. But in his fifty-seventh year it was an easy thing to fast . . . when food became a duty it was pleasure to neglect.

There was a muted glow, a kind of silver in the afternoon. The sun was pale. The snow still lurked beneath the shrubs and in the shadow of the tower. The gravel sounded crisp beneath his feet. He stood outside the rectory for a moment, and a deep nostalgia filled him, as if he had stayed from home too long. He entered by the front door and closed it behind him. And still the yearning, the melancholy held him. All was quiet here. And it struck him as unfinished. He could find no other word. Unfinished, he thought. What is unfinished? This room? This house? Or myself?

Then he walked into his study, and there was Timothy, sitting before the model of the church and drawing something, squirrels perhaps, or kittens, on a blotter with the staff pen from his desk. The ink spread through the blotter in a line that would not stay a line, making creatures newly born, of a softness undefined, and growing . . . growing, till there seemed no lovely thing they could not finally become.

Timothy laid down the pen and looked up. And together they were held in growing softness, so much promise, linked by a line that would not stay a line. . . . The moment passed.

"Where would our lady be?" Tom asked.

"She's under here," said Timothy. He disappeared beneath the desk and rose with her against his chin. "She's getting pretty heavy." He dropped her carefully on the desk, and she walked away to touch the little tower with her nose.

"I wonder," said Tom, "if she would be content alone here for a while. I thought we might go out before I take you home. . . . Isn't there some shopping you would like to do?"

Timothy looked at him with questioning eyes.

Tom took out his billfold and touched it discreetly. "We are loaded," he said, "if that is the word. I believe it is. . . . Now, these cousins of yours," he began in a matter-of-fact way.

Despite the crowds, they found a football and a catcher's mitt, and a dollbed for the girl who was barely three; and for Timothy himself, a knife with seven appendages, which he was not to see again until the following morning. In a small voice that Tom could scarcely hear above the din of the store, he announced that that was all.

"Are you sure?" asked Tom, and he looked at the boy from the corner of his eye.

Timothy nodded gravely.

The crowd was suddenly, hotly between them. When they had fought their way together again, "Your aunt?" said Tom.

The boy looked down.

"Now, a scarf would be nice," and Tom shyly fingered a bit of blue chiffon. It was the blue the mother of Our Lord wore in the paintings. "Or something nicer—"

The boy looked up, his eyes dark and mute.

"Now, here," said Tom, and he drew them both out of the swarm at the counter. The outgoing wave bore them relentlessly toward the door and abruptly dropped them short of it before the window for display. "What would you like?" Tom began.

"You just give presents to people you like."

"Well, now," said Tom, bending down to be heard, "sometimes you do it, anyway, don't you? Maybe just to show you would like to be friends."

The boy looked back at him, profoundly troubled. "You have to be friends first," he said at last.

Behind them, the crowd had fallen back against the counters. At the limit of his vision, without turning his head, Tom could see a balloon Santa bobbing up and down above a whistling jet of air. Far behind, he heard a plaintive, shrill recording of a carol. Nearby, there was the tinkle of a carousel of whirling angels. He sealed himself against the frantic movement and the lights and the whistling and the tinkling and the jaded, harassed faces that swarmed beside him at the door. And he was suddenly sick at heart for the service at midnight, sick because he would not have it now to wipe away the vision and the sound of this folly. This jolly folly, he pronounced and closed his eyes. The image of Christmas has become this mass hysteria. Or am I older than I know?

Then he remembered that he was talking to a child, who must be kept a child this day. He studied his own ghostly

103

image in the plate glass, standing among the handkerchiefs and vases and trays.

"Why do we give presents?" he asked himself aloud. But he was asking them both, seeking the answer in the two reflected faces, as if they could be wiser than the flesh had proved to be. "Isn't it because at Christmas God gave Himself to us? And we are grateful and would like to give Him something in return. We can give Him our love, which is the best thing of all." He braced himself, for the child in the mirror was looking into his eyes. "But somehow we would like to give Him something we can touch, in the way . . . in the way we could once touch His son." And in the mirror Tom noticed with surprise that he had touched the boy beside him, but lightly, more than lightly, so that it almost had not happened.

The people behind them in the glass drew close, and for a moment Tom Beckett and the boy were lost among them. They watched the stranger-faces replaced by other faces that never saw the two of them, until these too were gone.

"Then we remember that He asked us—when He came and we were close enough to touch Him and to hear His own voice—that always He asked us to love one another." He closed his eyes against the faces before he could go on. "Now, that's something we can do. What's more, we can give to one another all sorts of lovely things to show that we love."

He looked long and deeply at the boy in the glass. "You're right," he said at last. "It's all wrong. It's all wrong to give if you don't love."

And it seemed to him that much of the sorrow of the world lay somehow hidden in this, that there were too many gifts when the giver bore no love. The gift is a lie—perhaps it is a curse—when the giver bears no love. And yet a world without giving! It is one of the reasons for loving one another, . . . that the sweetness of giving may belong to us again.

They were suddenly in league against these frenzied strangers with their sealed-tight faces and the money in their pockets and the lie in their hearts. "Shall we go?" Tom said at last.

And when they were outside, hunting for the car. "Timothy," he said humbly, "I am not at all the thing for you. Every Christmas makes me feel a little older and sadder. This year," he began, but he could not finish.

They drove home in silence beneath the garlands of many-colored bulbs above the streets, between the lamp posts, holly-wreathed, already lighted, waiting for the dark to appear. The sun was still above the tops of the houses.

Around the church the traces of the snow were shadowed over. The walks were shadowed over. And as Tom Beckett climbed the steps to the rectory, the shadow fell across him; the yearning, the melancholy struck at his life. And again, when he entered, all was quiet . . . and unfinished.

Timothy went off to find Cornelia in the study. Tom stood in the dusk of the living room and waited. "Unfinished?" he thought again. What is unfinished? Can it be this room? Or this house? Or myself?

Then the thought came upon him: I have been in this house for twenty-seven years, . . . and it may be that I have never lived in it before. And he would not think again but turned and walked into the study. And Timothy was standing before the miniature church.

"Is this where you live?" he asked, and he had found the place. And when he touched the window, Tom Beckett held his breath. The child had looked inside and seen him. For the moment, unbelievably, he was known to this child. The shock of it held him silent. Then, as if a hand that held his heart had been loosened, his loneliness seeped away. He rested,

105

strangely comforted, in the knowledge in those eyes. And he saw for the first time how the sorrow of his life lay in this: not that Katherine had died, but that she had died before the coming of this knowledge; that somehow her departure had broken that promise the earth makes to lovers, that one day, late or soon, they will be known to one another. . . .

"Is this the place where you live?" Timothy repeated.

"I think it is," he said. And at once inside Tom Beckett something quietly prepared to be finished. As if the heart of him would turn and face another way; and this was beginning.

But this is ending, he told himself. This is the last time. And he said aloud, "Are you hungry yet?"

He did not wait for Timothy's reply but turned away. Suddenly he wanted this given hour more than he had wanted anything for twenty-seven years. "Some bread and milk will be the thing," he said, and his voice trembled.

He walked through the living room into the kitchen. The late sun was striking the window of the transept and flashing it across the wooden surface of the table. The table was before him, scrubbed, and warmed with light. The linens, clean enough for God, were folded on the chair.

From the shelf above the stove, he took an earthenware pitcher and held it beneath the faucet to rinse away the dust. Then he filled it with milk from the refrigerator and placed it on the table in the light. He did it with a slow deliberation, as if for years he had prepared himself to fill this very pitcher and to place it so.

He turned back to the counter. And lo, in the bread box lay a stout loaf of bread freshly baked by Mrs. Travis; and he recalled her gesture of the morning, when with an air of mystery she had covered up the bowl at his approach. May God bless her, he thought. Perhaps three times a year she was moved to bake him bread as he had known it as a boy.

And again he was reminded that nothing came by chance, nothing happened to be. . . .

When Tom was ready for him, Timothy appeared and sat down at the table. Tom would have said a grace for them, but nothing that he knew, none of the customary words, would suffice. Perhaps it was because he did not yet understand if they came to eat and drink or if there was something else, . . . some word to be between them. Some sign. Some glance. And the bread, the milk to lie before them, whole, untouched. But essential . . . but essential for the glance, the sign, the word.

Then Timothy looked at him with the simple question. "Yes," Tom said aloud. And he was glad to say it; and so relieved that his hand was trembling as he reached to pour the milk and to take the loaf into his hand and cut it, as he used to watch his father cut it, with the great blade moving toward him, toward his heart.

He buttered the slices with care and said to Timothy, "This is the kind of bread I had as a boy." He paused. . . . He had almost begun to tell it—about the long days, the long, long days, and the going to sleep and waking the following moment to morning, and the tree where God lived every summer. And always, everywhere, it was morning—the long days, all of them, always morning. And the taste and the feel of the bread in his mouth. The feel of the bread in his hand in the morning.

And again, as he sat there, the yearning caught him, the nostalgia that had gripped him as he stood a while ago before this house. He was homesick for the time when there was nothing better than this, . . . for the time before he had outgrown this bread and filled his hands with holy things. Then, he had been as round and whole as this loaf before him. Then, there was in him, in himself, a simple nourishment. Then, he could have filled a man with hunger in his heart.

He watched the cheeks grow wide with it, the dark eyes catch and hold the sunlight from the window. On the small fingers were the smudges from the desk pen. And in the center of him began a kind of movement; a life that seemed to spring and grow within him from the bread, that would not be contained but went out from him and surrounded him, was in his lively glance and in the way he brushed his mouth, and could be more, could fill the room. . . .

He saw that Timothy had finished eating, and he reached for the loaf. "Consider diligently," the maker of Proverbs had said, "the things which are set before thee."

And suddenly, as he touched the bread, there was David asking for it and the priest of Nob replying, "There is no common bread under my hand, but there is holy bread. . . ." His own hand trembled as he took the loaf and cut it. No common bread . . . all bread is holy. The boy was watching him, and he looked deeply into the eyes before him. The boy took a long draught of milk and emptied his glass. No tentative sips, as if uncertain how good it was, how much was needed. All of it was needed now. Now it was good.

Tom lifted his own glass to his lips, and in his mouth were the words of Christ, as if he drank them from the glass he held: *Take, eat, . . . drink ye all of this.* The very words he would have spoken in the service at midnight, but now alive with meaning for this moment of his own. . . . *Do this, as oft as ye shall drink it, in remembrance of me.* As oft as ye shall drink it . . . as oft as ye shall take it, remember that each day God ate this food and made it holy.

Then he saw it in the face before him, that God Himself became a child and made all children holy . . . and grew to be a man and made men holy . . . and lived among the things of this world and made them holy. He laid his hand, palm down, upon the table. And before his eyes, the dishes on the shelves, the altar linens on the chair, the towels, the pewter urn, the bits of dust in the light, were full of meaning. It seemed that he had touched each single thing in the room with one swift movement of his hand and knew them all. The boy before him—he had touched this boy. The flesh that covered solid bone. Beautiful, justly made clean through. The bone of his spirit, the spirit of his bone.

He could not breathe because the words were all his breath: God Himself lived this life I live and made it holy. And at once a door had opened in the wall of his life, and he had walked through it into the open. And here there was neither afternoon nor morning, . . . only this moment made holy by Christ, who had lived like himself from moment to moment.

But, he cried silently, I must always have known this! How have I served God and not always known it? And then he remembered that there is a way of knowing and yet not knowing, and that sometimes we must become as a child that we may truly know.

He stood, because he must make some gesture, and walked to the window. Outside, the afternoon swung in the balance between day and night. The sun was beginning to redden the sky, and over the transept a moon hung waiting as pale as snow. Suddenly he recalled that Saint Francis had called the sun his brother. And in his mind were the words of the saint as if they were made for him long ago and held in keeping for him till now.

> Praise to my Lord for all His creatures; for our brother Sun who bringeth us day and light, and showeth Thee unto us.
> Praise to my Lord for our sister Moon . . . and for the Stars hung bright and lovely in Heaven.

It was as if, with the words, the sun and the moon and the stars were given. "Praise to my Lord for our brother Wind. . . ." He could not find the rest. "For our mother Earth who doth uphold and teach us. . . . Blessed are those who find themselves in Thy most Holy Will." And he thought with deepest wonder that he had known the sun for all his life, and that only now could he call him brother.

When he turned, he saw that Timothy was standing, and that Cornelia was drinking from a saucer at his feet. He said, and his voice was strange to him, "I'm glad you remembered our friend." They became the first words he had spoken in this house from a living heart.

Then the telephone was ringing in the study. It was someone from the Altar Guild alarmed about the linens.

"I shall place them on the foremost pew at once." He listened to his own voice as if it were another's. He hung up quietly. The books upon this wall had haunted someone else. This rug upon the floor, someone else had paced. This little tower, remote and secret in the faint light, someone else had climbed. . . .

Then it flooded back upon him, and again he was Tom Beckett in his fifty-seventh year, but sundered, . . . but at the mercy of more than his years.

Already it was deep blue twilight where he laid the linens in the nave. The porch alone he had lighted. It gave to the interior its own peculiar dusk. God? he said, and waited for a little. And then he was afraid and somehow glad to be afraid . . . and then afraid of being glad. But this, he knew, is how it is when we are friends with God and cannot live unless we please Him. He longed to stay among these things that he had always known were holy. Give me a little time, he prayed. My heart is very slow. . . .

He went outside again, where night had fallen. Fallen? But it was as if it rose to him and opened, and he entered.

"Timothy," he said, when he had gone inside the house, "I think we'll walk you home instead of driving. Put on the jacket, and we'll take the things we bought."

When the two of them were walking through the streets, Cornelia close at heel, he did not try to speak. Cornelia ran ahead and lost herself in midnight underneath the hedges, then returned to find his injured leg and, with a rare perception, refrained from loving it to pain.

The rising moon was shifting through the branches of the trees beside him. He had heard it said that after many moonlit nights, the living cells, the very substance of the trees, is altered. It seemed to him these trees were slowly changing and that he did not want them strange, that what he wanted was a cloud across the moon to hold them fast. He wanted everything beneath the moon held fast till he should know it and possess it. Yet it would not hold; . . . it would not wait.

He found that he was praying that he might be spared the parting. Let me walk away, he asked, as I have walked away before. But even as he prayed, he knew that, from this hour, in every parting he would leave this child. And when the house was just ahead, he knew as well that in this parting now he left Katherine again.

At the front steps, Timothy picked up Cornelia.

"Shall I go inside with you?" Tom asked.

Timothy shook his head and tipped the fur of the cat with his nose.

Tom laid the gifts on the floor of the porch. The wind swirled the dust from under the house. It smelled of a secret and barren world. In the lamplight from the window he saw how the face of the child was numbed. And he wanted to take all the memories he saw there and bless them. Or to give to him the memories of his own unhaunted childhood. For he found that they were all he had worth giving. . . .

"You going now?" the boy asked suddenly, and his voice was lost. He was slipping from the shoulder of the great-C bell and falling.

Tom turned to him. And for a moment, together they were falling down the tower . . . till with an effort he seemed to catch the child and hold him. Then in his heart, deliberately he stood aside.

From his distance, he groped for a word that would be for the child alone, . . . some phrase he had never made before, nor would make again. He had given his life to the making of phrases. His eyes were filled with the face of the child, and his mind with the cry: A half a century stands between us, yet both of us have run away. And how can I show the way home to him, when I have never found it myself?

In his mouth and his throat was the taste of the dust. He dropped his eyes to the still, gray form that the boy held between them. If there had been anything at all in the Creed to support it, he would have given this cat his blessing. Instead, he offered with a painful shyness: "I hope everything will go well with your friend."

The boy nodded gravely. "She's done it before. . . . That's the trouble, you see." And he glanced at the door of the house and back.

"Don't worry, . . . don't worry. The whole thing is settled." He sighed and looked down at the steps in the darkness. "If you have any trouble, of course, get in touch with me."

But the boy shook his head. "She won't have any trouble. She knows how to do it."

"I know. I know. But I meant with them."

The lamplight from the window lay along the hedge like snow. Someone was moving just beyond the door. Timothy said quickly, "I'll save you one. I'll save you the best one."

Tom looked away and into the hedge.

"Would you like a girl or a boy?" said Timothy.

After a silence, Tom could speak. "A boy, I think."

Timothy nodded. "Grown people generally do." Then he looked up at Tom, and he trembled on the brink of something. "The trouble with boys—" But he did not say it. Perhaps he did not know. He gathered the cat close with his arms.

Did he mean that, with boys, this miracle of life seemed to stop or was somehow transferred to a house down the street? His own life rose behind him. Katherine . . . and their unborn son . . . and this boy. Yes, this boy too was already in his past. And none of it had ever lived with him but had somehow been transferred to a house just down the street.

Timothy shifted the cat to his shoulder. At last he said it: "I lost your key."

Tom shook his head. "It's all right; it's all right. . . . It really wasn't my key."

"It wasn't? The way you sounded, I thought it was."

"I know. I know. It's the way I sound."

"I was keepin' it to give it back."

Tom nodded.

"So you wouldn't think I was just goin' to keep on keepin' it, you know."

"Yes, I know."

"I might could find it some time if I looked."

"You come back and look," Tom Beckett said. It was good to be given a reason to say it. He watched the boy going into the house, wearing the jacket from the box for missions.

When he turned and walked away, it seemed he left behind all Christmases to come . . . and that never again would the service at midnight crown his year. He said to the night, the stars, and the moon: Behold another wise man seeking the king of glory and finding the child in the stable.

So be it, he said. So be it. So be it. I have had my

113

Christmas. I shall go to bed. I have lived it wrong. I shall ask forgiveness; I shall go to bed.

But if God had wanted it another way, He would have sent this child to me a dozen years ago. . . . And suddenly it was sharp as pain in his breast that this day he had been granted a final taste of all the sweetness and the fullness, the length and breadth and height of this life that he had missed. In his fifty-seventh year, when it became too late for more. With the coming of this child he was given life, and with his going, it was taken away.

For the first time he understood the prayer of Christ in the garden. It was not alone the suffering and the sin He would take upon Himself, but with it, He cried out against the loss of all of this, all this life in deepest measure.

He walked without direction, but with a vivid sense of anguish that the night with all its stars, its look of snow across the moon, its haunted loveliness, retreated before him—its frosted rooftops lilac in the moonlight, its naked, sleeping trees, and in their branches black and waking shadows that drew back at his approach. The bodies of the trees, struck deep with many nights of moon, were changing, even as he passed, till they were strange to him and he was strange to them.

Far down the street, the lights of town retreated before him. And after a while it seemed that time itself was retreating. Or perhaps that he had used it up, as he had always said, until no more of it was left. Somewhere in his mind he found a fragment of a line: "Life you may evade, but death you shall not." And the cold was in his heart.

What had passed for his life had been words and stolen phrases, carefully arranged to make the sound of a life. Passages from Scripture fastened end to end, fragments from the poets, and a sermon of John Donne. And a small, synthetic fervor. And a long-lost grief.

114

A woman passed him with a shawl around her head and her bare white hands alive and moving in the darkness with the rhythm of her walk. Then a child came running, his breath a cloud beside him. And he longed to tell them: It still belongs to you. It seemed to him he was alone in grieving for the lost life, for they still possessed this life that he had thrown away. Life you may evade . . .

He found that he was walking toward the town, . . . that he could not bear the thought of going home. And as he walked there came upon him slowly, imperceptibly, a sense of waiting. His leg began to ache, and he told himself he only waited to find a place to sit down. Yet the feeling grew, as if it were a thing outside himself that surrounded him and drew him quickly on toward the lights, till almost it seemed that just ahead he was expected.

But his knee was protesting the unaccustomed action and the cold night air, and he glanced around him sharply. Before him, on the outskirts, was an ancient house that looked to be converted to a shop. A sign above the sidewalk read, "Coffee and Antiques." Through the windows he could see the fire on the hearth.

Tiny festive bells jingled when he opened the door and again when he closed it. He was standing in an entrance hall before a fair-sized room. At one end was the fire and a ship upon the mantel with holly in its sails. Around the walls were tables very close together, and people at the tables. He took off his coat and hat and hung them in the hall. Then he stood in the doorway. The room was faintly shabby, but the fire on the hearth became at once a part of all the world that he had lost.

He was led to a small round table in the corner set before a spinning wheel.

"I should like a cup of tea," he said, "if you have it. With milk. Yes, with milk."

"Anything to eat with it?"

He hesitated, thinking he would like to stay a while. "Perhaps a piece of toast."

"We have a little muffin that is very good with tea. Very light. Very nice."

"Just a piece of toast," he said.

The fire was warm against his aching knee, and he was glad to be no longer alone in the night, though the people around him seemed apart from him, remote, as if not one of them had noticed when he entered. He put his face between his hands to take the numbness from it. Then he could not even hear their voices, so far away they seemed, so enclosed in the circles of their festal warmth and light.

When the tea came, he sipped it slowly, gazing into the fire, letting it lap the edges of his mind till there was nothing past or present but only flame and shadow in the places of his life. This was the way it had been before the fire one Christmas Eve with Emma. The night that God had spoken in the darkness, "I am making you new," and he had come to know that all the world was made for him, and he in turn was made for all the world. . . .

Using firelight and memory and longing and dreams, he tried to call it back, that ancient knowledge. This night the world miraculously seemed made for him again, as it was in the beginning, as it had been all these years. Why could he never reach out and take what was his? Why could he not reach now?

And the answer was in the firelight, so terrible, so final: that he had not in truth been made for all the world, . . . that he was never fashioned for the ministry of God. He had more than lost his life; he had mistaken it.

The figure of a man shrugging out of his coat stood between him and the fire, and he closed his eyes. The bells on the door tinkled frantically and hushed. . . . To go astray is bad, yet it can be forgiven. But to mistake the voice of God from the very beginning is to lose life indeed.

A woman in a fur hat, who was sitting very close to him, leaned over and spoke. He could not hear her words, but her eyes were bitter. She seemed to be a little younger than himself. Although he did not want them now, he asked her to repeat her words.

She wiped her lips with a handkerchief, then she drew it down slowly, and the firelight was moving in the hollow of her throat. "Are you a minister?" she asked. She was staring at his clerical collar.

He inclined his head.

"I thought you were," she said. "Do you believe in God?"

He had learned long ago that drunkenness and bitterness are hard to distinguish. "Yes, I do," he said. For a moment he was lost in her small bitter eyes.

"I believe in Him too." She touched her lips again. "But I hate Him."

He looked away into the fire. With a single word the pain in his leg could spring alive.

"That shocks you," she said. "That makes you want to leave."

"No," he said; and after a moment, "but I'm sorry to hear it."

She raised her cup to her lips and looked at him resentfully over the rim, moving her eyes back and forth across his face, but as if each feature of it left her mind as soon as she had passed it. "This is Christmas Eve," she stated. "Are you happy about it?"

He did not answer.

"Do you know what it means to me?" She put down her cup. "It's the night I get drunk. . . . And then I come around here and sober up on this. And when I can climb the stairs, I go home and go to bed. What do you think of that?" she said.

He felt her coiled and waiting. He shook his head.

She began to wipe the tips of her fingers with her handkerchief, carefully, delicately, as if the gesture gave her pain. And suddenly her small bitter eyes were full of tears. She said, "I lost my only son on Christmas Eve. In the war." She pushed her cup away. "I sober up too fast."

She watched him with her eyes brimming over with tears, and they seemed to him the tears of the woman he had left behind him in the morning. And then they were his own, all the tears never shed for his own lost life . . . or for any other life, in twenty-seven years.

"You wouldn't understand," she said to him slowly. "Did you ever lose a child on Christmas Eve?"

The words had struck at him. He closed his eyes and nodded.

"You're lying," she said. "You're saying it to save my soul."

But he shook his head. He could not speak. And he watched her go on crying with an aching relief, as if she shed for him the tears he could not shed. He listened with a kind of love for her weeping. The firelight was pulsing like a living heart. He cradled the warm, empty cup in his hands. And suddenly he saw the bread that he had not touched. Slowly the murmur of her grief reached and filled it, till it seemed the sound of it must bless the bread and break it.

. . . This is my body which is given for you.

. . . There is no common bread. . . . All bread is holy.

All things are holy.

. . . All these holy things are given for you.

Take them . . . in remembrance of me.

He did not look up, for the room sprang around him with intolerable closeness, each thing intensely single in the beauty of its holiness: the spinning wheel behind him, the

118

firelight before him, the tables, the chairs, the very walls. He dared not see them, so full of Christ they were.

It seemed to him the woman must see it in his stead, for her tear-stained face held the beauty and the holiness around them in the room. And by a miracle, her son was his own; this unknown son—he had known him all his life. They mourned him together, this son and no other. So intensely they shared it that in the moment of exchange, their grief fell between them and lay among the things of this room. And they saw one another in the hallowed light of grief, freed by it, and free of it.

The single moment spread across Tom Beckett's life and changed it into another thing. He knew it was accomplished, yet he dared not believe it. He stared into his cup as if he held the past imprisoned in his hands. And there he saw his faith—deeper than the faith of the child who once believed—that for twenty-seven years, and for the whole of his life, he was made for all the world. He was made for this night.

He could not remember how he went into the street. He only knew that he was walking and a light snow was falling on his hands and his face.

. . . This is my world which is given for you.

In the shapes of trees and houses he beheld a tenderness. And each stood out, intensely single, as if it had been loved, . . . loved since the beginning, and given now in love. Beneath the ground he walked on, the waters of the rivers were following his course. Each step he took was final, was recorded. And he took the next in faith and began his life anew.

He saw the lighted streets, the smoke of chimneys rising, curving toward him, and the night sky curving over him, till he was sheltered and enfolded and given, finally, the greatest gift: the power to reach out and take it; given, greater yet, the power to be given, . . . to give himself to all that he received. All around it lay in wait for him, invading him, possessing him; snow filled, dark filled, light filled, Christ filled, and the morning stars were singing now together. At the corner he had stopped and was holding out his hands to take and be taken. His arms and heart were aching with relief in the gesture, . . . so easy, so well remembered, that he knew he had begun it many times before this moment. In the falling into sleep, . . . in the falling down the tower, he had lifted these hands.

The cars had halted for his crossing. He waited, for each act, he was aware, was made forever. Then he stepped into the lighted pathway. The snow was falling red-gold through the car lights. And it seemed as if a thing from heaven mingled with the substance of the earth, the very air, and gave it glory.

. . . See this, as oft as ye shall cross the street on a snowy evening in the heart of winter . . . in remembrance of me.

He walked on, upheld and surrounded by the night. As he turned a lighted corner, the wind sang against him as sharply and as clearly as a bell note in the tower. And on the bell note, borne upon it, blended into it, sustained: Praise to my Lord for our brother Wind. In the space of night the wind was sweeping clean of the snow, the face of a man loomed before him in the light. Who was he, then? He was not a stranger. Yet Tom was sure that he had never seen him or these others who met him now and passed him. He gazed at them all, these familiar strangers, and was amazed to find that he had known them all his life and that only now could he call them brothers. The wind swept the words down the street before him:

These are my brothers which are given for you.

And strangely, though they passed him and were lost inside the night, they walked with him still. He could scarcely believe it, what a company walked beside him. Timothy was there. The woman he had left before the fire was there. And at last he suspected, and then he was certain, that Katherine was among them and had always been among them. There had always been this company of those he had loved. It had seemed all along that she was lost in the night, that she had once passed him by, like his brothers in the street. But now he rejoiced in her, ... rejoiced in the love he had had all his life, and had at this moment . . . and had at this moment.

He stood quite still in the falling snow and felt the joy of life invade him, as he had not felt it since he was a child no larger than the boy he had left just now upon the doorstep; yet greater joy, greater that he had denied it down the years, dammed it till the floodgates broke.

. . . This is my joy which is given for you.

There fell upon him, like the snow, the words of John Donne, . . . "He can bring thy Summer out of Winter, though thou have no Spring," . . . made for another Christmas, and made tonight for him. Beneath his coat, he touched the words that were folded in his pocket. And there he waited while they flowered in his hand, with the snow against his face and the full green of summer leafing surely in his heart.

Standing in the warmth and fullness of his season, he heard the bells, and he saw, almost laughing with surprise, that he was home. Before him was the church, and the crowd was going in. At once he was aware that he had come here to join them. Looking down into his heart, he saw that it was so.

He did not go in at once, but waited outside just beyond the circling light to watch the others go inside. All his life before, he had stood in that doorway, when everything was over, and watched them depart, had seen how they left him, till the last one was gone. Tonight it would be different. He

121

would see how they entered; he would walk in and join them, it seemed to him forever.

He waited, listening to the bells; for the first time hearing life in them, hearing "Christ has been born," and hearing — for they rang away his pride and his humility — "Tom Beckett has been born." And wonderful to tell, he heard the sound of William, higher pitched, a little shriller with his English voice. It was part of all the world that had been lost and restored. For in these singing moments when his birth was proclaimed, all losses were his own, and all restorations were made this night to him. In the bells there was the echo of that birthday long ago, when he walked about and waited to know the thing he most desired. And here at last the day itself had been returned. And he was asking for this night.

The others had gone in, and the doors had been closed. The bells were silenced, and the music began, and the voices joined the music, but still he did not enter. He waited for the late ones, blessed be they. In the past, he had always been impatient with the late ones. Late for God, he had said. But now he loved the world that detained them, the world they brought with them, trailing clouds of it behind them as they passed through the door.

He waited because he had come late, very late, to God's world, and he must love it a little longer before he left it outside. . . . Even so, he knew that when he finally went in, he would only be entering that world a little deeper.

Still, he went on standing just beyond the circling light, until at last he understood that he was not to join them. For in the afternoon, he had given it up. Yes, . . . yes, he thought, and waited in the silence. I gave it up for this night. It was the best thing I knew.

And perhaps, in exchange for it, the world had been given. Who could say it had not? And the answer was the echo:

Blessed are those who find themselves in Thy most Holy Will. . . .

His knee was whispering a little chant of pain in his heart, and he began to feel the cold in his face and in his fingers. He drew the collar of his coat around his ears and turned down the gravel walk on his way to the rectory. The windows, glowing, shimmering with candles, threw their shafts across his darkness.

When he passed the final window, the transept was before him, and the door into the tower. And suddenly he was thinking: If this door should be unlocked . . . Surrounding it, the fingers of the ivy caught the snow. Slowly he removed his glove, the better to know the latch, as if it held for him a sign. He felt it give beneath his touch. And pausing yet again, he thought: If I should go inside and the door into the transept should be open as well . . . The ivy spilled a little of its snow upon his hand.

He went into the tower, and the door beyond was open. Here, the light was like sunrise, so warm and pale it was. He stood among the racks for choir vestments. They were empty of the robes, except for one that once had covered the tallest man who ever sang, and through the years was kept hanging here in case he should return. The choir still could laugh to see it, for those who sing freely, laugh freely, he had found. And in a sense, they loved it, or loved the thought that it was here.

He walked to the solitary robe that swept the floor where it hung. When he touched it, far away he heard the voice of Bill Ryder. He drew in his breath. He took a long time to form the words in his heart: Don't leave me, Bill. Then he said them with his lips till they were almost a prayer.

This is why I came, he thought, and would have turned to leave. But suddenly a mighty voice of prayer was sweeping toward him. He clutched the robe beside him to brace himself against it. And he could not leave that voice, . . . the voice of all his people, . . . the voice of all his world. He clung to the robe; he hid his face in its folds. And the voice became his own, . . . giving God the glory for all that He had given.

When it released him, he turned and opened the door into the tower stairway—for tonight no door was locked to him—and dropped upon the foremost step, unable now to leave. And the warm breath of the church, the breath from God's altar, rushed past him up the stairway and through the ringing chamber, where the names of children waited, and up into the clock room where he lay on the floor. On the floor of the clock room, a part of Tom Beckett, which never yet had risen, cried out to join the others here below in praising God.

Their mighty praying voice called out to him again. He heard how, within, they rose, advancing to the altar. And in the clock room overhead he rose and descended, for it was as if they lifted him into their warmth and movement, into the grave and joyous march, the measureless journey, lovely among candles, where the white and gold was rising from the singing silence and all things were being born.

God made sun and moon to distinguish seasons, and day and night, and we cannot have the fruits of the earth but in their seasons: But God hath made no decree to distinguish the seasons of his mercies. In paradise, the fruits were ripe, the first minute, and in heaven it is alwaies Autumne, his mercies are ever in their maturity. We ask our daily bread, and God never sayes you should have come yesterday, he never sayes you must againe to morrow, but to day if you will heare his voice, to day he will heare you. If some King of the earth have so large an extent of Dominion, in North and South, as that he hath Winter and Summer together in his Dominions, so large an extent East and West, as that he hath day and night together in his Dominions, much more hath God mercy and justice together: He brought light out of darknesse, not out of a lesser light; he can bring thy Summer out of Winter, though thou have no Spring; though in the wayes of fortune, or understanding, or conscience, thou have been benighted till now, wintred and frozen, clouded and eclypsed, damped and benummed, smothered and stupified till now, now God comes to thee, not as in the dawning of the day, not as in the bud of the spring, but as the Sun at noon to illustrate all shadowes, as the sheaves in harvest, to fill all penuries, all occasions invite his mercies, and all times are his seasons.

John Donne
Christmas Day, 1624
St. Paul's Cathedral